"You don't really know me, Charley."

Kit's quiet warning was alarming. "It's only a few weeks ago that we first met."

"You don't know me, either, for that matter," she reminded him sharply, her face slowly flushing as he continued to stare at her. "Maybe you're going to regret this."

It was really tricky to try to sound threatening when he was hovering above her like Nemesis, and the idea of being married to him, having to face him day after day, was quite alarming, to say the least.

"Not me, Charley," he told her quietly. "I know exactly what I want."

She just went on staring at him, uncertainty in her eyes. Her gaze was drawn to the firm lips even against her will.

"It's nice to know that you don't find me utterly repulsive," he said softly, drawing her close as his head bent to hers.

PATRICIA WILSON used to live in Yorkshire, England, but with her children all grown up, she decided to give up her teaching position there and accompany her husband on an extended trip to Spain. Their travels are providing her with plenty of inspiration for her romance writing.

Books by Patricia Wilson

HARLEQUIN PRESENTS

934—THE FINAL PRICE
1062—A LINGERING MELODY
1086—THE ORTIGA MARRIAGE
1110—A MOMENT OF ANGER
1125—IMPOSSIBLE BARGAIN
1150—BELOVED INTRUDER
1174—A CERTAIN AFFECTION
1198—WHEN THE GODS CHOOSE
1221—THE GATHERING DARKNESS

HARLEQUIN ROMANCE

2856—BRIDE OF DIAZ

PATRICIA WILSON

temporary bride

Harlequin Books

TORONTO • NEW YORK • LONDON
AMSTERDAM • PARIS • SYDNEY • HAMBURG
STOCKHOLM • ATHENS • TOKYO • MILAN

Harlequin Presents first edition January 1990
ISBN 0-373-11238-6

Original hardcover edition published in 1988
by Mills & Boon Limited

CHAPTER ONE

WALKING to work, Charlotte admitted to herself that she had a king-sized chip on her shoulder about Sanford Petrochemicals, but it was only natural. She frowned at herself in a shop window. At this rate, she was going to be lined and anxious-looking before she was much older.

Of late, her uncle Joe had been worried more deeply than ever about their financial position. Maybe it really was because he was beginning to feel guilty that he stayed at home while she worked; after all, he was not an old man. Still, he knew how things were. He had been injured in his job and now he was unable to climb and move with the skill needed in the oil business. He had been lucky to escape with his life when the oil well caught fire.

It was unfortunate to say the least that the only job she could get close to home was with the very same firm. The new offices of Sanford Petrochemicals had been built here in the town instead of in the city, and she supposed that it was cheaper for them to operate here, certainly the building land was cheaper, and she was grateful for that because there were no other jobs in the district, otherwise she would have left.

The new offices had been completed just as she had finished her course at college, and she had been proud to work there, until Uncle Joe had been forced to retire early with a badly injured leg that had now left him quite lame and with no pension at all! Charlotte had found that disgraceful, utterly unthinkable, but he had shrugged it off. Sanford Petrochemicals were not, it seemed, a generous firm, and they had blamed him for his carelessness.

It had given Charlotte the rather big chip on her shoulder about her employers. Uncle Joe was her only relative. Her mother had died four years earlier and they had always lived with him since her father's death when she was five. Charlotte had always called his cottage home, it was the only home she could remember.

That he was now no longer able to work didn't matter very much. Charlotte was well paid and Uncle Joe owned the cottage outright. What did matter was that any mention of money was beginning to upset him badly, and as he should have had compensation for injuries, let alone a pension, it did nothing to improve Charlotte's private opinion of the firm.

Problems! Problems! Uncle Joe hadn't helped this morning, either. He had moved the morning's mail almost by sleight of hand. His 'Nothing!' when she had asked what was in the morning's post had been very evasive, and she knew that there would be new bills to pay, something that he would brood over privately while she was at work.

'Good morning, Charlotte!' One of the local policemen nodded to her as he walked past, giving her an admiring but fatherly smile.

She was good to look at, although she didn't feel it this morning. The sunlight caught the shine in her thick, brown hair. Her grey eyes usually smiled, but now they were a little too thoughtful. She was in her 'office mode', her smart blue suit and white blouse, the sort of brisk image that pleased Mrs Atkinson, the office manager.

'Good morning Mr Reynolds!' She smiled, her beautiful face lighting up enchantingly, quite making

Police Constable Reynolds' day, but the smile couldn't last. She was too worried; a deep feeling inside her urged her to turn and walk back, to have serious words with her uncle.

Mrs Atkinson would have been shocked, however. Charlotte was never late and never inefficient. Mrs Atkinson would have been seriously overworked without Charlotte. She relied on her, had relied on her since Charlotte had started with the firm when she was eighteen.

She beamed at the speed of her shorthand and typing, at her no-nonsense attitude in the office and, at twenty-two, Charlotte was considered to be the office manager's right-hand woman. No, she couldn't be late. Uncle Joe would have to be given a talking-to when she got home tonight.

She approached the junction of the road with thoughts of her uncle still roaming around in her head, the rapidly mounting bills to pay, and it was only because the feeling that something was wrong suddenly grew on her that she became alert enough to see that there was going to be an accident and that there was absolutely nothing she could do about it.

A large black Mercedes was coming along the High Street towards her, the driver unable to see what Charlotte could see so clearly. Another car was about to turn into his path, the driver of the second car making no attempt to stop at the 'Give Way' sign. It happened with the inevitability of a dream in slow motion and, although neither car was going fast, the nasty sound of metal on metal told her that somebody had a badly dented front wing. The Mercedes!

It would have been an exaggeration in this town to say that a crowd gathered, but Charlotte was not the only one to stop, and by the time that the drivers had recovered sufficiently from their surprise and shock to get out of their respective vehicles, at least ten people were looking on with interest.

It was a very big man who climbed slowly and purposefully from the Mercedes, not big in the sense that he was a huge man, but tall and powerful, broadshouldered. And the way that he rounded the bonnet of the car with long, swinging strides to survey the damage, his hands on his lean hips, his jacket open and pushed back, had a menace of its own that made Charlotte glad to be merely a witness and not an eager participant in this drama.

Every movement deliberate, he looked across at the driver of the other car, who was by now examining the radiator of his well-polished Ford.

'You feel like explaining this?'

The Mercedes driver was an American, Charlotte could hear that at once, his low, drawling accent adding an additional menace to his tall, tough appearance. The small but interested crowd perked up expectantly, a couple of other people joining them, and the American glanced across in irritation.

He had blue eyes, Charlotte noticed, cold, clear blue eyes that looked as if they were narrowed to look into the sun or out across the desert. It was a hard, lean face, deeply tanned, with not one ounce of softness in it. There was no give in this man, and the narrowed eyes swung back to the driver of the Ford with a pitiless determination.

'I'm sure there are plenty of people here who saw what happened,' the Ford driver blustered. 'Being an American, you'll not know the rules of our roads very well, but even so, if you're driving here you should make some attempt to learn them.'

He looked appealingly at the crowd and got no help

there. They were both foreigners, and it mattered not one bit that one was from the other side of the Atlantic while the second was probably from the next town; a foreigner was a foreigner. They stared back blankly and settled in to enjoy things.

'Could you all move along, please, unless you happen to be a witness!' Police Constable Reynolds had obviously heard the nasty-sounding crunch and turned about. He was there suddenly, with authority in his voice, and the crowd dispersed rapidly, more worried, Charlotte thought, by the idea of being a witness than by the authority of the local policeman. She stayed.

'Now, then . . .' Notebook at the ready, Police Constable Reynolds prepared to solve the problems, but the Ford driver was determined to get his word in first.

'This chap came along . . .'

'Just one moment, sir. Let's get this sorted out in an orderly fashion. Name, please, sir?' He looked at the American who was very clearly about to come to the boil and was just managing to keep his impatience under control.

'Landor, Kit Landor!' The long, firm lips snapped shut on the name and the policeman looked up expectantly.

'Would that be Kit as for Christopher, sir?'

'No! It would be Kit as for Kit!' He suddenly turned a baleful eye on Charlotte. 'Haven't you got better things to do with your time, young lady?' he snapped.

'Oh, hello, Charlotte! You'll be late for work.' Police Constable Reynolds noticed her now and turned to her in surprise.

'Business before pleasure, Mr Reynolds,' she said,

her face cool and efficient-looking. 'You asked who was a witness. I am! He nodded and turned back to the American who now looked closely at Charlotte, no doubt wondering if she was as efficient as a witness as she appeared to be from her appearance.

'Your address, Mr Landor?'

'At the moment, seventeen Beauford Terrace.' Again the firm lips snapped shut and Charlotte pursed her own soft lips. Beauford Terrace, an expensive area, luxury flats, still, he did drive a Mercedes.

She watched him, fascinated, as the policeman took details of the other man and methodically wrote them down. She had never seen an American before, except on the television. This one looked hard enough to be a very awkward customer, and the narrowed blue gaze that turned from time to time on her made her shiver a little, but she stood her ground, her face locked into its business like mould, fatalistic now about the fact that should would be late.

'Now, then, Charlotte. Just tell me what happened as far as you could see, and then I'll let you get off to work. I don't need details from you about your name and address,' he added with a fatherly grin. 'Just tell me in your own words.'

Difficult to tell him in anybody else's, Charlotte thought wryly, but she began without preamble.

'I was walking towards the junction, just after I'd passed you, and I saw the Mercedes coming along the High Street. I wouldn't have particularly noticed, except that I also saw the Ford approaching the major road and I could see he wasn't about to stop. He was going fast and he didn't brake. He just came out, straight into the road, and hit the Mercedes.'

'This American was going like a bat out of hell!' the

Ford driver protested loudly, appealing to the policeman and then glaring at Charlotte. 'You're making this up! You . . .'

'Watch that tongue!' The American suddenly seemed to gain about a foot in height as he straightened up and made a menacing movement towards the enraged man. Already very tall, he now seemed to tower over the policeman, and the Ford driver fell silent.

'Will you sign your statement tonight at the station, Charlotte, or shall I bring it along as I pass your house?'

'I'll drop in after work.' She smiled pleasantly, preparing to leave.

'It's a put-up job! You all know each other!' The Ford driver was beside himself with rage.

'Listen, you fruitcake . . .' The American was not in any way calm himself, and the policeman intervened hastily again.

'I think you can go too, Mr Landor,' he said quickly. 'As nobody was hurt, it will be a matter for the insurance companies. I'll just put my report in.'

'Well, if you want me, I'll be at Sanford Petrochemicals for the next few days,' the American said, turning back to his car.

'Fancy that!' The policeman looked as if there had been a minor miracle. 'That's where Charlotte works. All this has made her late.' He looked at the American expectantly, and the cold blue eyes turned on Charlotte.

'I'd be very pleased to give you a lift,' he offered politely, not looking particularly pleased at all, but she found herself being helped into the car, a hard, firm hand on her arm, and before she could think they were ready to move off.

'Thanks for your help as a witness,' he said gruffly, and Charlotte turned to look at him, her chin tilted imperiously. If this was an example of Americans, then she didn't like them very much. His manner was not gracious, to say the very least.

'Not at all. It's a civic duty.'

He shot her an unbelieving look and then turned back to the street, signalling and pulling out into the sparse traffic.

'Are you from the head office?' Charlotte asked inquisitively as they moved away down the High Street. He looked as if he must be. There was that cold air about him that smacked of the cold-blooded ways of the firm. She got a puzzled look and then a sigh of exasperation. Clearly he was still annoyed about the accident.

'Yes, the head office.' He was not about to say more, and she watched the cool face for a second, fascinated by its hard good looks. Quite sure that *he* would fit in very nicely with the general ambience of Sanford Petrochemicals.

'You're very brown. Do you normally work on the rigs? There's not a single rig in sight here, except the model in the general manager's office,' she said with an air that she hoped was superior.

'I'm an accountant!' he bit out stiffly, adding with a sarcasm that Charlotte thought was unwarranted, 'I spend a lot of time on a sunbed.'

'That's interesting,' she said, quietly annoyed. 'By the by, I can see that you haven't been in the town long enough to get orientated. We're going the wrong way!' She could hardly keep the glee from her voice, but she managed it. This American needed to be put firmly in his place!

'Why the hell didn't you . . .?' He glared at her and

then swung the big car round in the road, heading back in the opposite direction, the fast manoeuvre giving Charlotte a small fright, almost dislodging her cool manner.

'You did a U-turn in a forbidden area!' she informed him in an outraged voice, and gained for herself another glare.

'I'm not very civic-minded,' he assured her tightly, adding nastily, 'I bet you're really good at your job.'

'What makes you think that?' she enquired tartly.

'You'd have to be!' he informed her with a sour glance at her appearance.

It annoyed her immensely. It really didn't matter at all what this arrogant and bad-tempered American thought of her, but there were people going to offices every day who looked like this because it was expected! In any case, she was very smart! She wondered what his idea of a secretary was.

'As a matter of fact, Mr Landor, I *am* very good at my job, as you'll find out if you are to stay here for any length of time,' she informed him sharply. 'You will also find out that the offices run smoothly and efficiently, and that they are run by intelligent and well-mannered people. I really don't know how you'll fit in, but if you're only here for a short time perhaps they'll not notice your bad temper. Of course, it may be that you're here to bring our attitude into line with that at head office. It's going to be difficult. We take a more humanitarian attitude here!'

He slowed down to glare at her and then, without warning, he threw his head back and roared with laughter, his whole demeanour changing as if by magic.

'What's your name? Miss Prim?' he asked with a wide grin, his teeth vividly white against his tanned face.

'My name is Roberts, Charlotte Roberts,' she said, realising that when he stopped being amused he would probably make a note of her insubordination. It would be awkward to say the least if she too was dismissed, but she was unable to stop feeling annoyed.

'Roberts?' he murmured in a quiet, musing sort of way, as if it was an unusual name. Maybe he thought she had made it up on the spur of the moment?

'So, you work for a poor firm, Miss Roberts?' he asked quietly.

It gave her a pang to hear the edge of steely interest in his voice. There was no humour there now, but she refused to back down. He might be an accountant, but his lean, tanned face spoke of oilmen, and she had no soft spots for those, not after the way Uncle Joe had been treated.

'A mean, tight-fisted firm!' she said soundly, taking the bull by the horns.

'You're underpaid?' He shot her a slanting, keen-eyed glance, and she looked back coldly.

'I am not! I'm paid the correct rate and I expect no more. I wasn't thinking about myself!'

'I see! You're the trade union representative!'

'I'm nothing of the sort!' Charlotte said tightly. 'I was thinking of someone who was very badly treated by Sanford Petrochemicals, but as it's none of your affair, I'd be grateful if you'd let the matter drop!'

'Gladly! An argument is the last thing I need on my first day in a new town. This morning I've had two!'

The silence that filled the car all the rest of the way to the offices could only be described as bad-tempered. Charlotte could almost hear it, and she was glad to see the back of him, jumping out as the car came to a halt.

'Thank you for the lift, Mr Landor,' she said with a frosty smile. 'Have a nice day now!' she added in a fair imitation of his accent, some devil getting into her suddenly.

'It's been an experience,' he assured her bitingly, his eyes narrowed and angry, rather frighteningly blue. She would have to learn to curb her tongue, Charlotte thought. After all, she and Uncle Joe were very vulnerable; she just couldn't go around saying what she thought, and Kit Landor was from head office, that unfeeling place in Houston where Brett Sanford, the millionaire head of the firm, wielded power without justice.

She hurried off, giving him a quick glance, looking rapidly away at the angry glitter in his eyes. She suddenly felt very self-conscious, well aware that his eyes were burning into her back, taking note of the smart suit, the shining swing of her hair.

'Damn!' She had merely drawn attention to herself, and that sort of attention was the last kind she needed. He would probably want to photograph her so that she never got another job with the firm.

She ran quickly up the stairs, disconcerted to find that she was not thinking about being late, but about the deep American voice. She tried to remember the exact inflection, but she couldn't now. She could remember, though, how those far-seeing eyes had glittered with annoyance, and she wished she had left the accident when everybody else had. She wouldn't then have had this encounter with him. So much for civic duty! She hoped he wasn't staying here for very long.

She was exactly on time, and Mrs Atkinson gave her her usual look of approval.

'To the very second, Charlotte!' she remarked,

glancing at the clock. It was a temptation to tell her about the accident and how very nearly she had been late. It was also a temptation to warn her that there was someone even now parking his Mercedes who was a special envoy from head office, but it was not good image-making material and, in any case, it might look to the American that she had rushed in to warn Mrs Atkinson, as if they all had something to hide. She took off her suit jacket and hung it up, beginning work at once, taking up where she had left off yesterday.

He never appeared, and after a while she became absorbed in her work and the sound of the deep, angry voice left her head, so that it was with a feeling of great alarm that she looked up later in the morning to find him striding into the office with the general manager.

Mr Briggs looked a little ruffled, but the American had evidently regained his temper and, to Charlotte's relief, he merely nodded politely, giving no sign that this morning they had shared an unusual experience and harsh words. Still, for him it may not have been so unusual; certainly he didn't seem to have been shocked by the accident, merely enraged, and it hadn't taken him long to be enraged with her, either. She nodded back coolly and typed on.

'Ah, Mrs Atkinson!' Mr Briggs went towards Mrs Atkinson's desk, his busy manner clearly covering unease, Charlotte thought, watching carefully, her fingers still rapidly working. 'This is Mr Landor, from head office. He—er—he's the—er—chief accountant. He'll be here for a few days. Give him all the help you can, will you?'

'Why, certainly, Mr Briggs!' Mrs Atkinson shook the hand that the American offered, her face pinkly surprised, her well-coiffured white hair looking even more stiff. Charlotte hastily looked away as the American turned cold, blue eyes on her, her brief but fervent prayer answered when he said nothing, and she made a mental note to hold her unruly tongue in future. Attention from this hard-looking man was the last thing she wanted.

And what did Mr Briggs mean? 'He's the—er—chief accountant.' An odd way to introduce someone of importance to the staff! Unlike Mr Briggs.

Attitudes were the general subject under the hammer in the canteen at lunch time, and Charlotte was intrigued by the many variations of opinion about the mysterious American.

The general consensus was summed up in two words—hard and dangerous.

'Why dangerous?' Charlotte enquired, granting the 'hard' with no reservations.

'He's a snooper!' one girl said firmly.

'A sort of company hit man!' was another opinion. They were all from out of the district, and Charlotte wondered where they had gained the sort of insight to be able to recognise snoopers and company hit men. She thought it was more than likely, though, coming from Sanford head office. She hoped the files didn't turn up anything about her. Still, how could they?

In any case, she suddenly found herself alone at a table as the others took their trays to a corner table to gossip, but her solitude did not last long.

'Mind if I join you, Miss Roberts?'

She actually jumped at the sound of the deep American voice, and without waiting for her answer he slid into a seat opposite, briskly setting out his lunch, pushing the tray to the end of the table. The canteen was suddenly very silent, and Charlotte felt very much under the spotlight.

'Shouldn't you be in the executive dining-room?' she asked in a low voice, leaning towards him. She hated to see anyone make a fool of themselves and, in any case, she wanted to get rid of him, but he glanced up with an unconcerned air that told her that he knew exactly where he was.

'No! Part of the job, Miss Roberts. I have to see that things work and that the money is being well spent. Tell me, what do you think of the canteen?' He stared across at her and she would have liked to duck her head to escape the keen, narrowed eyes, but she faced him firmly, even though she knew this was some sort of subterfuge either to pry into her own private affairs or to get to the bottom of the remarks she had foolishly made this morning.

'It's—er—very good. I eat here most days. I've no complaints.'

'Do you always sit alone?' he suddenly shot at her with an alarming change of tactics, but she still looked back calmly.

'Mostly. The others are not from my office, and in any case, they're from out of town. I think those three there have a flat together in the next town, so they know each other well.'

'Don't you know anyone?' he pried quietly. 'Or is it this small-town thing, all strangers unless born here?'

'Well, that's true in a way,' Charlotte agreed, 'but as to not knowing anyone, I know everyone in the town. I was born here.'

'Where do you live?'

'Is that another question on your list of enquiries?' she asked with a cold glance at him. 'My address is on file.'

'Actually, that was an attempt at normal conversation—maybe I'm a little rusty at small talk.' He turned his attention to his meal, and Charlotte's heart went back to a normal beat. He *was* prying into her affairs!

'I live at Lilac Cottage, at the far end of town,' she said stiffly. 'I'm sorry to be so suspicious but, well . . . you're a little alarming!'

'I'm alarming you?' He smiled slightly, his hard lips quirking. 'I didn't think that anybody could manage that. You're a little alarming yourself with your civic duties and your efficiency. What's alarming about me?'

'Only everything,' Charlotte said with a tight little smile of her own, wondering how the conversation had turned like this. Maybe she was misjudging him? Was he actually attempting to be friendly? She supposed that he must be extremely lonely in a town like this. There was really nothing to do if you didn't live here permanently.

She wasn't about to take any chances, though. She looked at him haughtily, trying to make him go quickly. This was a great strain, and she had quite enough to contend with. The workload at the office was very heavy at the moment, and her own worries were never too far from her mind. Kit Landor, with his probing questions and his far-seeing blue eyes, was undermining her in a very annoying way.

She found herself staring at him, blushing furiously when she realised it, and she looked away rapidly as he said quietly, 'Obviously I'm bothering you, Miss Roberts. I apologise. Enjoy your lunch.' He left the rest of his own lunch and walked away, leaving Charlotte feeling guilty, rather mean and most definitely worried.

After that, she hardly saw him—well, not to speak to. All his questions were for Mrs Atkinson when he was in her own office, and although he was in her office very often he never spoke to her, and she kept her head down every time she heard his voice.

It was not until Friday that she actually met him face to face again, and that was when she was taking her lunch break in town, a little treat that she allowed herself every Friday. It gave her the chance to look in shop windows and sometimes to order groceries for the weekend to be picked up later.

She was in Willoughby's, the only decent department store, sniffing the latest perfume and trying it from the tester, when the voice spoke almost in her ear. 'Not your style, Miss Roberts. Too heavy.'

She looked round and a long way up into two cool blue eyes, and he smiled wryly, acknowledging unacceptable interference, but she made a great effort and smiled up at him. Better to have the devil on her side, she thought. She would just have to watch her tongue.

'Quite right. I like light, flowery perfume. Now I'm regretting the impulse to try it. I'm stuck with the smell of it all afternoon.'

'If you'll have lunch with me, you can wash it off right away,' he said with a rather offhand arrogance that made Charlotte's blood start to boil. He didn't mean it at all, she could see that, and she had no idea why he had said it.

'Why, I'd love to!' She summoned up every ounce of charm to confound him, and he did look startled, but only for a second.

'Good! We'll eat here!'

'It's rather expensive here,' Charlotte cautioned, quitely furious with herself for letting her temper land her in this.

'The expense account can run to it,' he assured her

ironically.

'How will you put me on to your expenses?' she asked with a fair imitation of Mrs Atkinson's manner, but he smiled down at her, his hard lips twisting in amusement.

'Secretary and business lunch, naturally,' he remarked, taking her arm and moving to the stairs that led to the top-floor restaurant. It was quite alarming, this feeling of being captured, but, after a few frantic seconds of thought, Charlotte decided there was no way out of it. Once again, she had talked herself into a corner.

Afterwards, she couldn't remember exactly what they had talked about. One thing she did know, though, he had got her to talk easily and she had told him just about everything that concerned her private life, although she'd had no intention of doing it at all. He ended up knowing about the cottage she shared with Uncle Joe, how she and her mother had lived there since her father's death, her school life and her secretarial excellence. She also recalled later that she knew not one thing about him, but it had not seemed obvious at the time.

At any rate, the time passed so quickly that she suddenly looked at her watch with an expression little short of horror and uttered the fateful words, 'I'm late!'

He was right beside her when she walked into the office to face Mrs Atkinson's scandalised eyes, and he spoke before anyone else.

'My fault that Miss Roberts is late, I'm afraid,' he said with a really charming smile. 'I bumped into her in town and insisted on taking her to lunch. It's a little boring, not knowing anyone here, and I'm just too friendly, I guess.'

Mrs Atkinson looked doubtful at that, and
Charlotte only just managed to keep the shock from
her face, but he was, after all, from head office, and
Mrs Atkinson managed a smile. She looked worriedly
at Charlotte however, when he had gone and
Charlotte was very industriously getting her work
finished. Could he be a philanderer? A close study of
Charlotte's businesslike face, her immaculate
appearance, eased her mind, but she felt a great responsibility for the girl. After all, she *had* trained her
herself to this peak of excellence.

'I do hope that he wasn't—er—well . . . ?' Faced
with it, she didn't quite know how to put it.
Charlotte, however, looked up at her with one of
those sensible smiles.

'Oh, goodness me, no, Mrs Atkinson! He really is a
rather lonely figure, I think.' She assumed a rather
motherly attitude, stifling the urge to add that no one
deserved loneliness more. 'He only wanted to talk.'

'He wasn't questioning you about the office,
Charlotte?' Mrs Atkinson said, realising a further
worry. 'I mean, we really have no idea why he's here.
Mr Briggs seems to be very much on edge.'

'No, it was just general conversation. You know I
wouldn't be so foolish as to talk about the office, Mrs
Atkinson,' Charlotte said briskly. 'Anyway, we have
nothing to hide—this must be the best-run office in
the entire Sanford Petrochemical empire!'

'Yes, you're probably right, Charlotte!' Her worries
cleared, she nodded happily at Charlotte and went
back to her own desk, but the worries were with
Charlotte now.

Just why was Mr Briggs on edge, and what exactly
had she told Kit Landor about herself? Had he been
probing into her background? She sighed and put the

idea out of her mind. Of course not, why should he? She was small fry for anyone like him to bother about. No, her first assessment must have been right. He was just downright nasty, trying to catch all of them out, that was why he had encouraged her to talk, and she was never slow to talk when she felt comfortable. It came from being too friendly.

She felt another twinge of astonishment when she realised that she *had* felt comfortable with him, even though he had spoken very little except to urge her on to talk about herself.

Uneasiness flooded through her but, even so, when he asked her to lunch again on Monday, she felt obliged to accept, if only to keep his mind off other things, admitting that he was quite exciting to be with, just so long as he didn't look at her too closely with those narrowed and probing blue eyes. He would probably be out of the country soon, and she had so far been able to talk to him without any slip. He must really be desperate for company, or very short of clues. She had even found herself boring because this time she had been on her guard, watching what she said until the conversation had become a sort of game, with neither player willing to make a false move. She had been left, too, with the distinct impression that he had found it all very amusing, although those firm lips had smiled very rarely!

CHAPTER TWO

AFTER two weeks, Charlotte could hardly say that she knew Kit. He was quite unbending, and she had no doubt that if he passed her in the street and had something better to think about he would simply ignore her. He ignored her in the building. She got the same brisk nod that everyone else got, and Mrs Atkinson's eyes became less watchful. She was quite sure that Charlotte was not, after all, about to be led into unseemly behaviour which would bring discredit to the office.

Charlotte had never even thought of it. Kit Landor was like a rock face. It was a little like knowing a distant mountain. Oddly enough, though, she had started looking forward to seeing him, without actually knowing why.

On the Wednesday, after another luncheon date with him—she had decided that it could loosely be called that—she was leaving the office when Mrs Atkinson actually ran a few steps to catch her.

'Oh, Charlotte! Will you do me the most enormous favour? I couldn't really ask anyone but you. I know that if you say a thing will be delivered it most certainly will be delivered!'

She looked most embarrassed, and Charlotte smiled reassuringly.

'Certainly, Mrs Atkinson. What did you want delivering?'

'Well, it's this file. Mr Briggs asked me to take it,

but I'm in a great hurry tonight. I know that it really is my responsibility, but I'm going to dinner with my brother and his family, and if I sidetrack, I'll miss my train. Mr Landor has gone and he needed this file. He's going tomorrow so we shan't see him again, but I don't expect he'd like to go without this. Can you drop it off at his hotel, or whatever? The address is somewhere here . . .'

Charlotte was stunned. She stood there and let Mrs Atkinson find the address, although she knew it perfectly well herself. He had said it at the accident and she had not forgotten. He was going tomorrow and he had never mentioned it! Not even a civilised goodbye! He was simply going without a word. It amounted to rudeness in her book!

'I'll take it!' she said a trifle frostily, and Mrs Atkinson glanced up sharply.

'You don't mind, Charlotte?'

'Of course not! It's on my way home, actually, I'll see you tomorrow, Mrs Atkinson.'

It was not Mrs Atkinson's fault that she was disappointed in Kit Landor, and she admitted to herself with surprise that she *was* disappointed. She had started to get used to him, to his ways. She had begun to make excuses for him, and she had to admit, too, that the role she played was dull, being careful all the time about what she said. She had probably bored him out of his mind. It was quite likely that after lunch with her he needed a stiff drink! Still . . .

Beauford Terrace was in a very good part of town, the houses modernised but not modern. They had at one time been townhouses of rich people, and even now, when they had been converted into flats, they were still only for the people with money—nobody else could afford the rents. Of course, Kit Landor had an unending expense account.

She found number seventeen and rang the bell. It was the lower floor and she heard him coming at once; even so, she jumped a little when the door opened. His height always took her by surprise.

'Charlotte? What on earth are you doing here?' He sounded a little irritated, and she almost pushed the file at him.

'You forgot this! Mrs Atkinson asked me to call on my way home. She couldn't come herself.'

'Well, thank God for that!' he murmured vaguely, his eyes on the file. 'I wouldn't know what to do with a woman like that.'

'I'll be off, then. Goodnight.' Charlotte turned away, quite anxious to get out of range. He hadn't even said 'thank you' for bringing the file, and she felt very irritated. If she didn't make a quick getaway her tongue might just lead her into trouble again.

'What?' He still had that vague look in his eyes as he glanced up from the file, and to her astonishment he took her arm and drew her inside. Even so, she was fairly sure that he had no real idea that she was there.

'Do you want me to wait for a message or something?' she asked hurriedly as he propelled her into a warm sitting-room.

Indoors, in a normal house, he looked a lot bigger and a great deal more hard. She was used to seeing him in a suit, but now he was in more casual wear and he didn't look at all like an accountant. He looked like a man who lived a hard life, a man who was quite accustomed to taking care of himself. It was like having a tiger in the living-room, and she suddenly found herself a little anxious.

'You want to make some coffee, Charlotte?' he muttered offhandedly, his eyes skimming the papers rapidly as he sank into an easy chair.

'Er—do you want me to?' He looked up at her, his narrowed eyes so blue that they were a little dazzling.

'What? Oh, yes, please.' He looked away again almost immediately, and she did think of telling him that manners maketh man, but her sense of humour came to the surface and she looked round to find the kitchen, hoping that Americans liked instant coffee with no fancy preparations.

He was deeply absorbed in the file and its contents when she came back with a tray of coffee, and she poured a cup for him, finally getting his attention by holding it almost under his nose.

'Oh, thanks!' He looked away and then muttered, 'Sit down, Charlotte, take your jacket off. I like to be warm. It's damned cold today!'

'It's going to rain,' Charlotte ventured, hoping that it would not rain until she got home, still wondering why she was waiting. Of course, she knew that she had entirely slipped his mind by now!

'Well, these are good!' He finally put them down and looked at her. 'Did you type them?' She glanced across and nodded, recognising the papers and remembering them.

'Yes. I did them this morning.'

'Not one error—you're good!' He looked at her steadily and she felt her face flush.

'Yes, I know,' she said, lifting her chin proudly. 'Mrs Atkinson said that you needed them particularly as you were leaving us tomorrow.' There was the edge of reproof in her voice and he looked quite startled.

'Tomorrow? She's got her wires crossed. I leave next week, not this. I'm going on Tuesday or Wednesday—I'll let you know.'

He was not then simply going without saying goodbye. Charlotte was horrified at the wave of pleasure this announcement brought, and her face flushed quickly, making him look at her closely, his eyes narrowed and assessing.

'Well, I'll be getting along home, then, if that's all you wanted,' she said quickly, looking rapidly away when his eyebrows rose in surprise. What a stupid thing to say! What else would he want? 'I can't understand Mrs Atkinson making such a mistake,' she added quickly.

'Oh, well, goodnight, then!' She made her way to the door and he walked politely to open it for her. She stepped outside, and he suddenly grinned at her, as he rarely did, his teeth white against his tanned face.

'Goodnight, Charlotte. Thanks for the coffee. See you tomorrow.'

She nodded briskly, keeping very tightly in her role of Miss Prim, striding out into the gathering dusk, hoping that he wasn't looking at her. He had this probing gaze that sometimes seemed a little *too* probing. She always had the feeling that he was after something, although she had given up the idea that he was prying into her affairs. It had just happened that she was the first person he had met here.

He was going next week! The very thing she had prayed for when he had first come. Now, the thought was not to her liking. She realised with a feeling of shock that she would miss him. In his hard and uncompromising way, he was exciting. Nobody like Kit Landor had ever been here before, and she did not imagine that he would ever be here again. She stepped out quickly. It really was going to rain.

When she put her key in the lock, nothing happened. She tried again with exactly the same result, and then she really began to worry. Uncle Joe had been worse than ever lately. He hardly ever went out of the house, and he seemed to be sunk into some morose debate with himself for most of the time. The cheery man she had grown up with was entirely gone. Suppose that . . .

She hammered on the door and was greatly relieved to hear his voice at the other side of it.

'Charley? Is that you?'

'Of course it is! Who else would it be?' She looked at him in astonishment when he drew back the bolt and let her in. No wonder her key had been useless!

'What are you doing with the bolt on the door?' He only looked at her worriedly, and she could see that this was going to take some time. 'Hang on! I'll get changed and then I'll give you a good talking-to!'

Charlotte ran upstairs and flung her jacket on the bed, slipping out of her skirt and tights and pulling on her blue jeans. She was just unbuttoning her silky blouse that she had worn at work, when a queer feeling of anxiety hit her. He was very quiet! She hadn't even heard him go to put the kettle on for her!

She raced downstairs, tucking her blouse into her jeans for now, an unaccustomed feeling of dread spreading through her.

'Uncle Joe?' Coming into the kitchen suddenly, she caught him off guard, sitting with his head in his hands, utterly unlike any way she had seen him before in her life. 'What is it? Uncle Joe! What's the matter?'

He raised his head, and his face was a mixture of fright and shame. He seemed to have aged ten years since this morning.

'We're in bad trouble, Charley,' he said quietly and miserably. 'Honestly, I don't know what to do. I've brought you to this, I've brought you down to my level!'

'I'll make some tea and then we'll talk,' Charlotte said quickly, feeling totally inadequate in the face of such words, but he stopped her as she moved away.

'It's no use, Charley! I've finished both of us off!'

Charlotte sank into a chair, surprised to find that her legs were shaking. She had no idea what he was talking about, but it must be something serious to affect him like this, and she watched his face anxiously.

Suddenly, without even knowing his problem, she was very worried herself. She no longer felt businesslike, efficient and calm. Her role seemed to have gone with her suit. She felt that she should be getting ready to tell him that this was all silly, but one more look at him told her that it was not.

'I think that whatever it is,' she said firmly, 'you'd better tell me—now.'

'I'd better tell you the lot, Charley,' he said mournfully. 'I should have told you ages ago, but I always hope. That's exactly the trouble, always hoping!'

'What—what were you hoping for, Uncle Joe?' she asked in a voice that she tried to keep businesslike.

'The big win! That's what keeps fools like me going. We wait for the big win!'

'You—you've been gambling?' she asked in an appalled voice, and his head sank into his hands again as he nodded.

'For years, Charley!' he confessed. 'Now, though, I've really finished us off. We're penniless!'

'That's nothing new lately!' It was like a weight lifting off her head. 'Uncle Joe! I work! I get well paid! We're not going to starve, and we've got Lilac Cottage. We'll manage.'

'No, we haven't got Lilac Cottage, Charley,' he said

bitterly. 'I took out a mortgage to settle my debts, but I never did. I tried for one more big win. We have nothing at all, not even a house.'

'Oh, Uncle Joe!' She suddenly felt terribly vulnerable, lost as she had not felt lost since her mother's death. It was no use feeling like that, though, and she pulled herself out of it. 'We can just keep on paying the mortgage. It might make us short of cash, but it will mean that we have a house. Maybe I can get an evening job?' she added hopefully.

'It's not even that either, Charley. They want their money! They want it now!'

'Who? What are you talking about?' She had rather alarming pictures in her head of the bank, or wherever he had obtained a mortgage, coming in a body to throw them out. Every word he uttered seemed to make things worse, and now there was a real fear growing to add to the stunned feeling she already had.

'I used to gamble when I was on leave,' he said dejectedly. 'I had plenty then, and they knew it. Often I gambled for more than I had, but they were always paid and I got a good name in the club. They let me place bets by phone since I've been injured. They don't do that for many people, not unless you've got a really sound financial backing.' There was a touch of pride in his voice that quite horrified Charlotte. To her way of thinking, it was nothing at all to be proud of.

'I went through the money I had,' he confessed, 'and bit by bit, I lost it all. They wanted paying and I couldn't pay, so I got a mortgage on the house to pay them off.' He looked up, his face drawn and frightened. 'I thought I might make it all back and then pay off the mortgage, so instead of paying them, I just gambled more and they let me. Now they want

it. They rang today, and God knows how they have
the number! They'll come, Charley! They'll come and
take this place apart, us with it!'

'Who are they?' Charlotte asked, jumping up, her
voice a mere whisper in her dry throat, the whole
point of this hitting her now.

'The boss is George Mellini—he's Maltese, I think,
but I'm not sure. He'll not come himself though, he'll
just send some men.'

'I'm calling the police!' Charlotte moved
determinedly towards the hall and the telephone, but
his really terrified voice stopped her.

'No! For God's sake, Charley! If you do that, they'll
kill me!

Charlotte realised that her heart was racing with
alarm. Not one hour ago she had been a secretary—
supremely efficient, with no great problems. Now she
was preparing to barricade the doors, cower inside
and expect some thugs to attack both her uncle and
herself. It was astonishing, difficult to believe, but it
explained his recent behaviour, his desire to stay
indoors. She had to get some help because the picture
he painted was not to her liking at all. If these man
came, then no sharp tongue was going to be enough!

She ran through the people she knew, discarding
them as each name came into her mind. The males she
knew now seemed like boys, not one of them over
twenty-three, small-town boys at that, with no
experience, none of them street-wise. Their reaction
would be exactly like hers—get the police. Of course,
it would be all over town, too, if she told anyone, and
then her Uncle Joe would never go out of doors again.

Quite suddenly a hard face came into her mind and
she could see the naked aggression in it. A rather
harsh, low voice seemed to be ringing in her ears. She

was back at the accident and watching Kit Landor's face as he looked at the man who refused to admit liability for the crash. She had watched him many times since then, and had sometimes shivered at the narrowed, cool blue eyes. The tiger in the living-room! There was a man who could cope with anything!

'I'm going out a minute! Lock the door!' She dived into the hall and grabbed a jacket from the hall stand, not even sure if it was hers but not caring much, determined to take action before her uncle could stop her. Pride would have to go to the wall here, not only her own but her uncle's as well. He was in a state of nerves that threatened collapse, and she could not in any way cope with a bunch of tough men intent on violence. To sit and cower behind locked doors was not her style, and in any case when she went to work, her uncle would be alone. Help was needed and nobody seemed more likely than Kit Landor!

'Charley! Come back here!' Her uncle was rather hampered by his leg and there was no way that he could catch her; all he could do was shout to her from the doorstep, and she turned as she left.

'Lock the door!' She had no doubt that he would, he was terrified!

At first she walked calmly, assuring herself that this merely needed a good hard head to solve the problem. But it was dark, the rain just beginning and within minutes she began to run, telling herself that it was to escape a soaking, but knowing deep down that her uncle's fear had transmitted itself right to her. By the time she came to Beauford Terrace, she had been scared by every tree, every bush. There was not a soul in sight. Normal people were having their evening meal, and she hoped that Kit Landor had not gone out for *his* meal.

She had a stitch in her side, and as she ran the length of Beauford Terrace the rain began to come down hard. Before she got to number seventeen it was simply pouring, and she almost fell up the steps, hammering on the door, quite convinced that 'they' were in fact chasing her even now—the darkness, the gathering wind and the hostile, lashing rain building up a feeling inside her that was quite alien to her normal reactions.

For a second Kit didn't seem to recognise her, his face puzzled as he squinted out of the light into the darkess and pouring rain, and then he suddenly gasped, almost dragging her inside.

'Charlotte! What the hell are you doing out there? You're soaked to the skin!'

She tried not to gabble, even taking a minute to get her breath, but when she started to speak it all come out wrong and he took her arm, forcing her into the sitting-room.

'Calm down!' He peeled her wet jacket from her shoulders, not that it had done much good, she hadn't even waited to fasten it. 'Sit there!'

He pushed her into a chair by the fire and she started to explain calmly that it would get wet from her clothes, but he looked as if he was about to swear, so she said nothing more and he walked quickly from the room.

When he came back, he pushed a thick towel at her and nodded to her hair.

'Get dry!'

Quite forgetting where she was, Charlotte towelled her hair vigorously, looking up with a flushed face, her hair a mass of unruly waves around her shoulders as he held out a drink for her.

'Now! Let's have it! I imagine you have a reason for

tearing round here in the pouring rain?'

'Yes,' she agreed, utterly mesmerised, watching him in some horror. Now that she was here, she felt utterly stunned by what she had done. Whatever had brought her to Kit Landor? She hardly knew him, was wary every time she saw him. Why, even just a little earlier she had been downright alarmed at being here alone with him!

He was just staring at her with those cold, blue eyes, and she took a great gulp of her drink, almost choking on it, trying very hard to pull herself back to normal.

'For God's sake, stop looking at me like that!' he bit out angrily. 'You're the one who raced here! What did you come for, to make quite certain that I scare you out of your wits? And stop holding that wet towel in front of you like a shield!' he added in exasperation. 'I'll give you advance warning when I'm going to rape you!'

She had never heard his voice so hard and she looked away rapidly, jumping idiotically when he took the towel from her hands and flung it on a chair.

'I—I came for help.'

She put her trembling hands between her knees and forced herself to look up at him. He did not look pleased, and his eyes ran over her shivering figure. Her silk blouse was wet and sticking to her, and she saw his gaze rest for a second on the rounded contours of her breasts, very obvious against the wet silk.

'Finish your brandy!' he ordered a little more quietly. 'It seems to me that you're not the sort of girl to go to pieces for nothing. So, what brings you wet and bedraggled to see me at this time of night, and what the hell are you so scared about?' He watched her trembling lips for a second and then added sardonically, 'Apart from me, that is?'

Now, she couldn't tell him. He was no friend, and she wondered how she could have ever felt that he would help, or even how he could help. Tough he might be, but if her uncle's words were to be believed, then there was a whole gang of villains on the way here. One man was no match for that, not even Kit Landor, in spite of her faith in his iron-clad qualities and utterly ruthless soul!

'It doesn't matter. I—I made a mistake.'

'You mean, you imagined I was human and now you've discovered that I'm not?' he asked drily, and she shook her head vigorously, gulping her drink, shuddering as it hit her hard again.

'No. It doesn't matter, after all.' She stood, swaying a little but determined to keep her family problems to herself, vague plans forming at the back of her mind. He pushed her back into the chair with no effort at all. He did it with one finger.

'How far did you run?' he asked, his eyes narrowed on her face.

'From home.' Charlotte looked down frustratedly, knowing that she had placed herself in a very awkward position and that the only person likely to get the benefit of his hard character was her alone. The wild run had quite shaken her and he had every advantage. She suddenly shivered with more than cold, and it was a further worry when he sat opposite, crossing one leg over the other in an attitude of waiting.

'Right! You were running from somebody or something, and you were running to me. Let's have it!'

There was little choice unless she wanted to shout and scream and fight her way out of here, confirming his obvious belief that she was mad. She told him, right from the beginning, and he sat perfectly still, listening to her low, shaken voice, making no comment whatever. It felt like talking to a very indifferent stranger. When she had finished, he stood and leaned against the mantlepiece, watching her downcast head. She had never looked up once, and she knew herself that she was very different from the efficient Miss Roberts at the office. He probably thought she was childish, and she wasn't even quite sure on that point herself. It seemed to be pretty safe here in this warm, lamplit room; maybe her Uncle Joe had just panicked and passed it on to her. She had read somewhere that it was very easy to become involved like that.

'Why me, Charlotte?' he asked in that harshly deep voice.

'I—I imagined that . . . I thought—thought that you were friendly enough to help and—and you're the only tough man I know. I thought you'd know what to do. I'm sorry. I told you that I'd made a mistake. It seems quite ridiculous now.'

She stood and he reached out one long arm, grasping her wrist, pulling her forward.

'I don't think so. Unusual for someone like you, perhaps, but certainly not unheard of once you've stepped off one circle of living and on to another. Phone your uncle,' he said in a very quiet voice. 'Let's just set your mind at rest that he's still OK. If I phone, he'll think that I'm after him.'

She gave him a grateful look and then dialled the number as he stood tall and hard beside her. Her uncle answered at once, as if he had been standing right beside the phone.

'Uncle Joe? It's Charley. Are you all right? Yes, I'm fine, but . . .' The phone was taken from her hand and Kit Landor spoke firmly into it.

'Mr Roberts? Charlotte is a friend of mine. I'm bringing her home, and then I think that you and I had better have a talk. In the meantime, keep the door bolted. Don't open it unless you hear Charlotte's voice.'

He replaced the receiver, his eyes on Charlotte's suddenly glowing face.

'Right!' His eyes ran over her, his look suddenly very different. 'You and I will now deal with Uncle Joe.' He strode out of the room as she sank thankfully into the chair, not feeling quite so stupid as he was taking it all seriously, quite sure that her worries were miraculously over. He looked capable of dealing with anything and anybody.

'Put this on!' He came back as abruptly as he had left, tossing her a sweater. 'A wet blouse is one hell of a thing! I can do without high blood-pressure!' Charlotte blushed to the very roots of her hair and struggled to get the big sweater over her head and over her blouse as he watched her with narrowed eyes.

He lit a long, black-looking cheroot, staring at her until she began to worry all over again. Then he said in a very American way, 'Yeah!' Nothing more, just that, in a musing sort of way.

She looked up at him with startled, grey eyes, and was extremely surprised to see a smile lighten the rather grim countenance.

'I really don't know what to do. I mean, I can't just stay away from work to protect Uncle Joe. I really am the bread-winner now! But you see, they're sure to come for him, so I can't leave him alone.'

'It all seems to be pretty drastic,' he agreed, reaching down to haul her to her feet. 'I think that the first thing to do is to talk to your uncle.'

'I already have,' she murmured, putting her sudden

light-headedness down to the brandy she had swallowed so precipitously. 'I've told you everything.'

'Well,' he said slowly, his eyes on her rather flushed face, 'as I seem to have been selected to straighten you out, I think that I would like a word with Uncle Joe, all by myself!'

'You'll not get annoyed with him, will you?' she said quickly. 'He's already scared out of his wits and—and you're very alarming.'

'Yes! I remember that you once pointed that out to me. I'm an odd choice for a friend, don't you think?' he suggested drily.

'I really didn't mean to push myself on to you. It was just that . . .'

'Honestly, I know!' He led her into the hall and collected her dripping jacket, not offering to give it to her as he opened the front door. 'And nobody pushes themselves on to me, Charlotte! I find you a very intriguing study. I can hardly wait to have a word with Uncle Joe. He just about takes the biscuit!'

He grabbed her arm and they made a run for his car. It was still pouring, and she was glad she didn't have to run all the way back. Faced with reality, she had no idea how he could help, but he was tough and definitely could not be scared, and he was coming with her to the cottage. It had lifted her spirits to a point somewhere up in the clouds.

There was a long delay as they stood on the front step of Lilac Cottage, waiting for her uncle to open the door, and she felt very impatient with him. She had already spoken through the door, so he knew perfectly well that it was her. Kit Landor was getting wet, and it would not soften his considerable temper.

When they did get inside, her uncle Joe looked at his visitor as if he was as much to be dreaded as the men who were after him, and Kit Landor just stared at him with a look on his face that almost bordered on triumph.

'So you're Uncle Joe?' he said softly, his mouth twisted in a grim humour that puzzled Charlotte and worried her immensely.

'Yes.'

Her uncle looked a bit desperate, very embarrassed and Charlotte cut in determinedly. 'I'll make some tea, unless you prefer coffee?' she said briskly. 'Then we can decide what to do. Mr Landor will—will help.'

She knew she didn't sound too sure of that, and she had no assistance from her uncle at all. He just stood there looking at Kit Landor in a stunned manner.

'We'll manage without the drink, Charlotte,' Kit said, his eyes keenly on her uncle. 'You're still very damp, you look tired out and you've had quite a shock tonight. You get off to bed. I'll see you tomorrow and we'll have a talk. Meanwhile, your uncle and I will bat this about a bit and see what we come up with.'

It really was what she wanted to do, but she felt like a deserter and her eyes strayed to her uncle. He nodded in a very resigned sort of way.

'You get along, Charley,' he said in a very dull voice.

'You haven't had anything to eat!' she protested, and Kit Landor cut in irritably.

'Have you, Charlotte?' His blue eyes looked quite annoyed when she shook her head. 'Then get yourself a sandwich and take it to bed with you. Your uncle can get his own later.'

He appeared to be taking over the world, but then, she had invited him. She nodded and moved to the door, and he was there before her to open it, looking down at her with a really grim face so that his words surprised her.

'Stop worrying! Nothing is going to happen. I guarantee it.' His voice was really softened. There was hardly any of the harshness in it that she had got used to. 'And get that thick hair dried properly!' he added by way of an extra order as he gave her a small but definite push into the hall and the general direction of the kitchen.

He shut the door tightly, shutting her out, and for a second, for some reason, she expected to hear his voice raised, but she could hear nothing. There was an odd feeling that they were both waiting for her to get out of earshot, and a great temptation rose in her to put her head to the door and her eye to the keyhold. Only the thought of Kit's face if he should catch her as it stopped her from doing just that.

She was really tired, and if she didn't get her supper now she knew she never would. It was definitely the brandy! She never panicked under pressure! With this utterly erroneous thought to support her, she made a ham sandwich and went up to bed, finding that she could hear the quiet murmur of their voices. That was comforting. They weren't standing there glaring at each other, then. She could pick out Kit's voice and she fell asleep knowing that he was still there. Oddly enough, she felt very safe.

CHAPTER THREE

IT WAS early in the morning when Charlotte awoke to unexpected noise. Only momentarily disorientated, her first thought was that whoever was after Uncle Joe had in fact arrived. She didn't even pause to slip into her dressing-gown. She was scared, but the overriding feeling in her was outrage, and she exploded on to the upstairs passage in a fury. This might be a cottage that was now unexpectedly mortgaged, but she lived here, and so did her uncle!

Kit Landor was walking past her door, two suitcases in his hands, and for the first time since she had seen him he looked startled. For a second she did not find his presence in the cottage at all odd, but her aggressive stance and her wide and furious eyes stopped him in his tracks.

'What happened?' She came to a halt and stared up at him as he stood watching her.

'Not a thing! Hold the cavalry, there's not one Indian in sight!'

'I heard a lot of noise!' she said suspiciously, and he nodded, not looking at all contrite.

'Yeah! I dropped a box, sorry.'

It suddenly dawned on her that he had no business to be here, unless there had already been trouble, and she stepped forward.

'Did they come? Is that why you're here? Did Uncle Joe . . . ?'

'Nobody came. I stayed all night and your uncle is

42

leaving. There's not a single soul to fight, unless you fancy having a go at me?'

Charlotte put her hands to her cheeks, her eyes wide and puzzled on the lean, handsome face that looked down at her.

'I don't understand any of this! Where is Uncle Joe going and why did you stay and . . .'

'I could do with some breakfast,' he pointed out drily. 'I never explain on an empty stomach. I'm sorry that you're up so early, but you did get an early night last night, which is more than I did. If you can contain yourself for about thirty minutes, I'll tell you everything.'

'But . . .'

'How about getting dressed?' he enquired softly, his eyes sweeping over her satin nightdress, and Charlotte suddenly became all too aware of the figure she presented. Her thick brown hair was a mass of disordered waves, the thin straps of her nightdress were sliding from her shoulders, and she was standing barefoot in front of a man she hardly knew.

'Er—I'll—what do you eat?'

'Everything I can lay my hands on,' he murmured quietly, his startling blue eyes watching her stealthy progress back into her room. 'Just make whatever you eat and give me two helpings. Good works sharpen the appetite!'

She made it to her door and darted inside as he strode off downstairs. His car drove away and it gradually sank in that the cases were her uncle's, that the house was now silent and that wherever her Uncle Joe had gone, he was going for some time and he had not said goodbye. It was astonishing how her life had changed overnight!

She dressed in jeans and shirt. It was only six-thirty,

so there was plenty of time to get ready for work later, and something told her that Kit Landor would expect his breakfast to be ready when he returned. She brushed her hair and then hurried to the kitchen, deciding that as it was so early she too would have a real breakfast for a change. By the time that his car returned, she had the table set and everything ready to eat.

He ate silently and methodically, his eyes intent on his food, and she had the decided impression that he was putting off telling her anything at all.

'Now will you kindly tell me exactly what has been happening?' she asked with sharpness intended to gain his attention as he finished and sat back. 'Where is my uncle and what have you been doing?'

He looked at her across the table, his blue eyes intent on her determined face.

'A real English breakfast. The first I've had. It was good. Mind if I smoke?' She shook her head impatiently and he lit one of those black-looking cheroots that he seemed to carry about with him and leaned back again, still watching her face. He was putting off telling her about her uncle, and her heart suddenly began to beat too quickly, a great deal of the determination leaving her.

'You can tell me straight out!' she said in a gallant attempt at coolness. 'I'm not at all scared!'

'You're a poor liar. That beautiful face gives you away instantly.'

'I'm not beautiful!' she said sharply, not liking his patronising attitude, and earning for herself one of his rare smiles—a worrying thing.

'You're not sitting where I am,' he informed her drily. 'You leapt out of bed ready to do battle at six-thirty this morning looking better than any woman I know looks at seven in the evening when they're ready to face the world. There wasn't much of the Miss Prim about you.'

'Mrs Atkinson likes me to look—sensible!' she said firmly, wanting to change the subject.

'Like her? I can imagine!' he drawled sardonically.

'I don't normally talk behind anyone's back!' she said tightly. 'After all, Mrs Atkinson employs me!'

'Wrong, *Charley!* he said softly, his eyes narrowed and very blue again. 'Sanford Petrochemicals employ you, that mean, tight-fisted firm!'

It suddenly hit her all over again that he was, after all, from head office. She shouldn't be worrying about Mrs Atkinson, she should be worrying about the tight air of satisfaction he had about him this morning. He was giving her the feeling that she was sitting in front of her executioner.

'I'm really sorry,' she said with a great effort to sound contrite.

'Little liar!' His eyes flashed over her face lightly and then he stood, beginning to pace about, confusing her even more. 'Let's get to the business of your uncle. I spent a good part of the night on the telephone, genuinely grateful for the time difference between here and the States.' He suddenly turned on her with a quick movement that was wholly alarming.

'Your Uncle Joe has been a gambler for a long time. He's got himself into trouble wherever he's been, and more than once the firm has bailed him out of it! We're bailing him out again, on my say-so. It's the very last time! I've put him back on the books and he's just flown out. There's job in the States for him, providing that he keeps himself out of trouble!'

'Oh!' Charlotte's little sound of distress did not in

any way soften his expression. 'You—you knew him—before!'

'Yeah! I know Joe!' he said testily.

'It—it's very good of you . . .' Charlotte began, but he cut in ruthlessly, his eyes quite icy, all big business executive and no friend at all.

'It's not good of me!' he grated harshly. 'Your uncle is not a poor old man, he's not even old at all, and neither is he a greatly misunderstood one, so get all those thoughts out of your mind! I didn't do this for him, I did it for you, and not because I'm your friend, either!'

He sounded so scathing that for a minute her eyes filled with tears that she hastily blinked away, and although he noticed, the hard expression never softened. The way her uncle had spoken about his gambling with a small burst of pride made her feel that this was all too real, that he had always had this habit. Kit Landor was not in any way trying to make her feel unscathed by this. Clearly it was a family crime, and she was sitting here with almost equal responsibility.

'It's a hard world, Charlotte,' he rasped. 'Once out of this little town, there's a variety of big bad wolves waiting to eat anybody they fancy. One good turn for another. Your Uncle Joe is away and running clear. I need you, and I figure that you now owe me!'

'What do you mean?' She jumped up, wild thoughts careering through her mind, and his hands came down hard on her slender shoulders.

'Calm down!' There was a faint twist of amusement to his mouth, and she stared at it in frightened fascination until he sighed and shook his head exasperatedly. 'I'm not about to demand your virtue!' he said with a wry look at her flushed cheeks. 'You keep impressing on me that you have hitherto untapped secretarial skills. That's what I want. Everything I do is very confidential, and I need a secretary to travel with me, somebody who can't simply get fed up with either the travel or me, somebody who needs to be away from her home ground and needs to keep in my good books. That's you, Charlotte!'

'I'm not at all sure that I understand,' Charlotte said a trifle shakily, and he glanced at her bewildered face and let her go.

'Pour yourself some more tea, sit a while and think about it,' he said sardonically. 'I'm sure it will gradually sink in.'

She sat, anyway. Her legs were none too steady and she was stunned at his hard manner, her mind teasing away at the things he had said.

He had helped her uncle so that he could demand her services as a secretary wherever he happened to be? It made no sense!

'There must be, quite literally, hundreds of excellent secretaries who would jump at the chance to travel with you,' she told him with a puzzled glance. 'Why go to all this trouble just to get me?'

'I had no intention of going to all this trouble, initially,' he informed her. 'As it fell into my hands, I just made the best of it. I'm an opportunist!'

'You didn't have to help us!' She looked at him accusingly and he just looked back evenly.

'But I did have to help you, Charlotte. You came running to me as a friend. I could hardly refuse you.'

'And in actual fact, you're not a friend at all,' she informed him in a dull voice, turning away, still unable to come to terms with all this. His hands came to her shoulders again and he turned her to face him, his finger imperiously tilting her face to his.

'Really? I've taken on a gambler and made myself answerable for his good behaviour! So far there's been little sign of good behaviour from Joe Roberts! In any case, now that your uncle has gone, you're the only one left. I'm not about to leave you here to face the music. They still want their money and you have no way of keeping this cottage as far as I can see. Your uncle left only on the understanding that I would take you with me out of harm's way.'

'You could have said it like that before,' she accused angrily. 'Instead of making me feel trapped.'

'I've discovered that nothing comes easy, Charlotte, especially as far as women are concerned,' he said with a bitter twist to his mouth. 'I didn't want you refusing to come, and I don't have the time to hang around and protect you.'

'Would you have done?' she asked in astonishment, her eyes wide.

'What are friends for?' he asked drily, making her face burn with embarrassment. She had put him to a lot of trouble. Maybe he was insisting on this job for him to make her feel that she was not under too big an obligation? One look at his face, though, assured her that he wouldn't really bother about her finer feelings.

'Better get ready for the office, Charlotte. If we set off early, I'll have time to call in at my place and change. When we've got your part of this sorted out at the office, you can come back here and pack. In view of the problems you've got, we'll leave today instead of next week.'

'It—it's a lot of trouble for you,' she said worriedly, her cheeks flushed as she realised what a responsibility she had suddenly become to him. He was almost a stranger, and she didn't particularly like him. She was very much in his debt.

'No trouble, Charlotte,' he assured her coolly. 'Are you coming with me then?'

'Oh, yes, please!' She felt that she had to sound enthusiastic, light-hearted. 'I told you that hundreds of secretaries would jump at the chance.'

'I'll make do with just you,' he said with a smile that told her he was not fooled at all. 'Now, let's move!'

'He never said goodbye to me,' Charlotte turned at the door, her face puzzled again. 'I can't understand that at all. He's been so good to me.'

'And I think that you've been good to him, maybe too good,' he said sharply. 'As to saying goodbye, I wouldn't let him.'

'You had no right!' Charlotte stood angrily in the doorway, her grey eyes over-large in a flushed face, and that strange and confusing smile came again.

'He's an oilman, back on the job. Believe me, he'll thrive! As to having no right, don't forget that you invited me into your life, Charlotte. I may not be so easy to dismiss!'

She hurried out after one last glance at the hard, handsome face. It was quite frightening, as if she had whistled up the devil, given him a foothold in her life. What could she have done, though? At least her uncle was out of harm's way, and it would be a good idea to go along with Kit's plans for now. She didn't at all fancy staying to face the music alone.

Go along with his plans? Charlotte felt like giggling hysterically. She had no choice, not if she wanted to keep her job. He hadn't threatened her, but the threat was there in his hard face and his cold, blue eyes.

She began to change to her working image, her prim and businesslike Miss Roberts, knowing that as they drove to the office she would be passing people she had known all her life, and that they would be totally unaware that she was having to flee from brutal men who would take pleasure in beating her uncle and probably in beating her.

She had made breakfast for a lean, hard stranger, and as she walked downstairs and he greeted her appearance with raised brows and gleaming eyes she blushed, remembering that this morning she had careered out almost into his arms in her nightie. She tilted her chin proudly and the dark eyebrows rose even further. Why did she get this impression that he could see right through all her subterfuge? He was still a mystery to her.

They arrived at the office before Mrs Atkinson, and her face as she entered was quite stunned. It appeared that Kit had already been on to the general manager, because he too hurried in early, the unusual turn of events quite throwing Mrs Atkinson off her stride.

They were all hustled into Mr Briggs' office and, as Kit sat on the edge of the desk in an unconcerned manner, the bombshell was dropped on Mrs Atkinson.

'Mr Landor is leaving us today,' Mr Briggs said with a certain amount of relief in his voice. 'He would like to take Miss Roberts with him.'

'My goodness!' Mrs Atkinson looked scandalised, and the fact that Charlotte was blushing brightly did nothing to allay her suspicions.

'All perfectly respectable, ma'am!' Kit said firmly, rising to his intimidating height. 'I have a conference to attend and I badly need an efficient personal assistant. Miss Roberts has the necessary qualifications. I've made it my business to get to know her while I've been here, and I'm sure that she'll do very well. She's discreet and—er—most suitable,' he added with an approving look at Charlotte's smart appearance.

'It's exactly what happens when you train some-body well, Mrs Atkinson,' Mr Briggs put in very diplomatically, and the suspicion died out of her face.

'Well, I can bring Maureen up and get her training going a little faster. She should be able to hold the fort until Charlotte returns. How long will that be?' She was beaming at Charlotte again, who had suddenly become her special envoy, and Kit Landor shrugged non-committally.

'A week—two. It's hard to say.'

'We'll manage!' Mrs Atkinson smiled and more or less bowed herself out, not noticing the puzzlement and growing dismay on Charlotte's face. A week or two? They would all be waiting for her when she got back, laying siege to the cottage, and Kit would be in America. What about all he had said on the subject of his secretaries deserting him when they got tired of it all? She wasn't going to get the chance to desert—she was going to be tipped out precipitously!

He commented on her glum expression as he drove her back to the cottage to pack her things, and she held nothing back in her worried state of mind.

'I don't always tell the truth,' he shrugged, his eyes on the road, his hard, powerful hands on the wheel. 'Let your Mrs Atkinson get over this shock first. By the time two weeks are up, she'll be quite happy with Maureen. We can then proceed on our way with no hearts broken.'

'Maureen cannot replace me!' Charlotte said firmly, her chin lifting proudly. 'She is not as well qualified, and she doesn't have the scope!'

'Naturally,' he said quietly. 'That's why I chose you instead of Maureen.'

'You said you were taking me to get away from those men!' she insisted as they drove up to the cottage and walked inside.

'Sure! But as I said just now. I don't always tell the truth. Choose whichever explanation suits you best. Now, let's get cracking!'

He just walked into the sitting-room and picked up the telephone without so much as a by-your-leave and, after one very disgruntled look at his broad shoulders, Charlotte ran upstairs to pack and change.

The feeling of relief that she had made her escape predominated as they left for London, but other feelings swam around inside her. There was the uneasy thought that her uncle had been somehow spirited away in a rather sinister manner. It still did not quite ring true that he had agreed to go without saying goodbye. She just could not believe that he would do that. To Charlotte it seemed unspeakably selfish, and she had never noticed that he was selfish, even though he did get filled with self-pity from time to time.

There was also the startled and all-encompassing look that Kit had given her when she had come downstairs ready to leave the house. They had never actually been short of money until recently; at least, Charlotte had never known it. She had a very good dress sense and plenty of clothes.

She had decided to travel in a silky suit that was both lightweight and uncrushable. It was the palest coffee-cream colour, the short-sleeved top belted around her narrow waist, her shoes and bag matching the vividly green belt. She looked very young and slender, and her face grew rosy at the approving look in Kit's eyes.

'Unbelievable!' was his only comment, and after they had picked up his own luggage and driven off from the town he had very little to say at all.

He was now her employer, she decided. The friend was not there at all, if he ever had been. His motives were not at all clear, but she had the decided feeling that she had been hustled into all of this, and that some time soon she was going to wake up and regret it.

Kit drove skilfully and said nothing. Glancing at him from her eye corners, she admitted that he was a very handsome man in spite of his hard looks. He was superbly dressed, powerful-looking, obviously the envoy of an important firm. Her annoyance with that firm was not there now. After all, she had not known that her uncle gambled, had been saved more than once by Sanford Petrochemicals. And they were saving him now, thanks to Kit. In spite of her unease, her spirits lifted.

He slowly turned his head to look at her, as if he read her change of mood, and it gave her a sudden quiver of feeling that she could not recognise.

'Problems, Charlotte?' he asked quietly, turning his attention back to the road.

'No, it's rather thrilling!'

The words just burst out as she attempted to cover the quick and odd trembling that had come over her when he glanced at her so keenly. He turned and looked at her steadily for a second, his blue-eyed glance lancing over her face.

'Maybe! Enjoy it. You'll recover soon enough, I guess!'

'Recover from what?' she asked, her eyes puzzled on his sardonic face.

'The thrill of being young!' He turned back to the

road, and the quickening tingle of awareness died out of her. There was not much enjoyment in anything when you were by yourself, and he realised perfectly well that she was by herself. Kit was no more human that a computer!

'You'll need a couple of evening dresses,' Kit said in a cool, matter-of-fact voice as he stood later in her hotel room and checked that everything was all right. 'I never thought to remind you to bring them.'

'Which is as well,' Charlotte said shortly. 'I don't even have one. Evening dresses are not the sort of thing I would have, you know, and in any case, why do I want such things now? I'm a secretary.'

'Wrong, Miss Roberts!' he said with one of his rare grins. 'You are a personal assistant. Where I go, you go, and I go to at least two receptions while we're here. The evening dresses are a necessity. However, not to worry, you can get a couple easily.'

'I can't!' Charlotte assured him determinedly. 'I really don't have that sort of money. Come to think of it,' she added, 'I don't have any money at all. You dragged me away before I could even think of things like that!'

'No need to look so desperate,' he said with a caustic smile. 'You can get anything you need here, and as to the money, you're with me. Money's no object!'

'You know, they really are going to question your expense account when you start adding two evening dresses to it!' Charlotte said irritably. 'I can see that you'll be getting into trouble over me.'

'No way! You just leave it to me, although I'm not at all sure that I'm not already in trouble over you, Miss Prim!'

'Don't call me that!' Charlotte glared at him with a very stiff and aggressive look about her, and then the meaning of his words dawned on her. 'I'm sorry!' she relented. 'I expect you'll have some explaining to do about taking Uncle Joe on again?'

'Some.'

He watched her speculatively for a few minutes, and then tilted her determined chin.

'I expect to have some compensation for my troubles, however.'

'What do you mean?'

This time the breathless feeling was choking, and there was no mistaking the look in his eyes, a look that had never been there before.

'Oh, come on, Miss Roberts!' he said sardonically. 'You came running to me for a favour, even when you admitted to yourself that I'm almost a stranger. I came up with the goods! Let's work out your debt, shall we? I rescued Joe, gave him a job at some risk to my own, and I've plucked you out of danger. Not bad for a mere acquaintance!'

He just went on looking at her, and she felt her face begin to flood with colour. She had no doubts at all about what he expected as compensation. She had always known that he was hard, unfeeling, but this had never occurred to her at all. In an odd way she had trusted him almost from the first, but now she was faced with the reality that he was a stranger and that she was here with him alone. He was powerful, miles from his own country, able to do exactly as he chose!

'Well?' He moved the back of his fingers down her cheek, and a shiver ran through her that she could not in any way hide.

'I—I'm grateful!' she managed in a whisper. 'You know I am.'

'So how are you going to show it, Charley?' he

asked softly.

'I—I don't know!' she confessed a bit frantically. 'You wanted me for a personal assistant and I'm here. I'll—I'll do my best.'

'Charley!' He looked down at her with a mocking smile, shaking his head at her deliberate misunderstanding, knowing as well as she did that she understood only too well.

'Then I don't know what you're talking about!' Charlotte snapped out, holding up her head in some attempt to hang on to reality and bring him to his senses, but he merely laughed deep in his throat and cupped her head firmly, drawing her swiftly towards him.

'I'll show you!'

For a second she could not believe this was happening. Things like this did not happen to people like her, but the brilliantly blue eyes were staring into hers and his face was close, too close.

'No!'

Belatedly she began to struggle, but he had been quite prepared for that. His hand twisted into her hair, and his other hand grasped her wrists, iron-hard and merciless, forcing her arms behind her as he pulled her tightly to him.

'Let me go!' She had time to choke out the words, but no more. His lips, hard and punishing, came down on her own, forcing her head back until it rested against his arm, leaving his hand free to release her hair and move determinedly to her breast.

'No!' Her words were a muffled plea against his mouth before he forced her lips apart, silencing her.

Fear and anger, panic and degradation rushed through her. Unable to struggle, she had to submit to this assault, shame overriding all other feelings as she felt a whole tide of response rising inside her.

His fingers dealt swiftly with the bright green belt that encircled her waist, and distantly she heard it drop to the floor, embarrassed to realise that her breasts had swollen tight and hard as his searching fingers slipped the buttons that reached to her waist.

'No bra, Charley?' he murmured against her lips. 'You're a liberated woman?'

She had no time to reply or call for help. He began to kiss her determinedly now, his lips and teeth making quick biting motions against her mouth as his hand moved to cover her breast.

'That's beautiful, Charley,' he murmured. 'Not prim at all.'

Charlotte found that there were some things that could not be hidden. The response of her body was one, the shock of it another. He was attacking her! Assaulting her here in this quiet room, and her flesh was responding, out of control! She was aware that his ferocity was now subdued, his hands subtly arousing, his fingers almost gentle on her tight breast, skilfully caressing, bringing the hard nipple to excited life.

Shamefully, she wanted to melt against him, and there was nothing she could do to stop her lips from softening to his. She tried to move, to pull away, but his hand left her wrists, his arm tightening around her, pressing her closer as the wicked pleasure continued.

His mouth left hers to travel the length of her throat to her breast and take the hard peak gently in his teeth. It was a chance to cry out, to shout for help, but the only sound that left her throat was a low moan, even though his hand was moving over her thigh, dangerously soothing, moving closer to the secret heart of her every second.

'Beautiful Charley,' he breathed, his head raised from her breast, leaving it secure and throbbing in his lean fingers. 'Innocent, too!'

The quiet derision did more than anything else to bring her back to the present, to allow anger to rise over the aching need that was even now flooding her entire body.

'Innocence is not a burden, Mr Landor!' she managed to snap, acknowledging as she said it the utter incongruity of addressing a man so formally when his hand still caressed her breast.

'It's so thin on the ground though, Miss Roberts,' he assured her, laughter in his voice, 'especially when it's coupled with such wildfire response.'

'You made it painfully clear what you want as recompense for your help!' she said strongly. 'Was that satisfactory?'

She expected a blaze of anger but he let her go, watching with narrowed and amused blue eyes as she fastened her dress with hands that trembled and bent to retrieve her belt.

'It was quite satisfactory, Miss Roberts,' he said evenly. 'However, that's not at all what I want.' He moved to the door, glancing back at her flushed and astonished face. 'Five minutes and then we'll have lunch downstairs. You look—hungry! Don't keep me waiting, Charley!'

When she went downstairs, he behaved as if nothing at all had happened, and to her chagrin it irritated her out of all proportion to the crime. She should have been grateful that he behaved as if everything was normal! What did she want? Did she want him to remind her that less than half an hour ago he had practically ravished her in her room? She was losing her grip on things! She set her lips determinedly as he solicitously led her across to their table, and her eyes sparkled angrily at him as he spoke quietly and pleasantly.

'After lunch, go out and buy yourself some evening dresses,' he said firmly. 'And no misguided thoughts of saving money either; the firm pays!'

'Oh, don't worry, Mr Landor!' Charlotte's smile was as hard she could make it. 'I shall feel no compunction whatever, not now!'

'Then it was all worth while, Charlotte!' he said drily. 'Two birds with one stone!'

She didn't enquire as to what the other bird was, but he watched her flushed face with a great deal of satisfaction.

Over the next few days, Charlotte found that her job consisted of doing absolutely nothing. She had bought the evening dresses, spending wildly and, to her mind, extravagantly, but Kit had never even asked the price. He had merely glanced at them when she had defiantly shown him her small but costly collection. He ate dinner with her every night at the hotel but, as far as anything else was concerned, she might just as well have been here alone. When she asked in exasperation what her duties were supposed to be, he simply shrugged and said uninterestedly, 'Nothing as yet. Enjoy yourself!'

After her initial shock and outrage, and her feeling of real guilt that she was not earning even the cost of her breakfasts, Charlotte had discovered that he really meant it. Most of her day was spent wandering around like a tourist. What he did with his time she never discovered. He was there to collect her when dinner time arrived, and he was always superbly dressed. Sometimes they ate out, away from the hotel, but that was really all she saw of him, and gradually she almost forgot that this was not, in fact, a holiday.

He reminded her sharply on their fifth day. She had spent the morning at the Tate, coming back in time for coffee, amused to find that one of the other guests took the opportunity to sit beside her in the coffee lounge and strike up a conversation. He had been eyeing her all the week, and some perverse whim led her to encourage him. Kit's remark about her innocence still rankled, so she laid on the charm to watch its effect, secure in the knowledge that she could always run for it if the situation got too sticky.

'Miss Roberts!' The hard voice was very clear across the room, and Charlotte turned with a look of surprise to see Kit standing by the door, his strong legs planted firmly, his face like granite. 'If you could spare a minute to get on with your job?' he said scathingly.

To get on with her job! She almost called out to know which job that was, but he didn't look as if he would take it very well. She smiled encouragingly at her admirer and murmured her excuses, leaving in a very leisurely manner that clearly irritated Kit to the point of explosion. His blue eyes were intent on her face, and then dangerously narrowed as he looked across at her admirer. He waited very pointedly until she was close, and then took her arm in a punishing grip, as if she would run out of the hotel if he took his hand away.

'Get your notebook and come to my room,' he said abruptly when they had arrived upstairs, and she fled on rather shaky legs. He was quite intimidating when he was like this, and her burst of irritation at his abrupt way of gaining her attention had now gone, to be replaced by deep anxiety. She went along to his room with her notebook and pencil at the ready, her heart pounding almost out of control.

'Sit down, Charlotte!' he said gruffly, after glancing at her slender shape in her blue dress. 'This won't take long.'

She didn't say anything at all, and after one glance at her as she sat with her pencil poised he began at a great speed to dictate a letter.

It wasn't quite what she was used to. The speed was nothing, but the letter itself seemed to be in a sort of code. Even so, she got it all perfectly and read it back to him at her own insistence.

'I wasn't at all sure that I had got it, Mr Landor,' she said primly. 'It seems to be almost in code.'

'It is,' he said shortly. 'Address it to the Chairman, Sanford Petrochemicals, the usual address, I expect you know it?' She nodded in a very competent manner and he almost growled at her, 'Don't call me, Mr Landor! Kit will do nicely!'

'I prefer to call you Mr Landor, if you don't mind. You are my employer!' she said tartly, thinking that perhaps some formality might keep him as he was now, annoyed and therefore safe to be with. She earned herself another irritated growl.

'You'll damned well call me Kit!' he exploded. 'Every other secretary I've had has called me that, and they weren't supposed to be a friend! Who was that lizard downstairs?'

'I've no idea!' she snapped. 'I didn't actually catch his name, although I was greatly taken with his civilised behaviour! And the next time you want me, Mr Landor, please don't gain my attention so—noisily!'

For a second he looked as if he couldn't believe her tone and then his face blazed with anger.

'I don't just employ you, you sharp-tongued little witch!' he bit out. 'I practically own you!'

'You *do* have an elevated opinion of yourself, Mr Landor!' Charlotte said sarcastically, wondering inside with a rapid burst of fright why she couldn't hold her tongue. He had already demonstrated his opinion of himself!

She sprang to her feet as his expression changed from annoyance to speculation, but he was too quick, he was on his feet already and one long arm shot out to secure her tightly.

'Lesson number two coming up, Charley!' he said drily.

'I'll scream the place down!' This time she struggled at once, but to no avail. He was always one jump ahead of her.

'In that case . . .' His mouth captured hers, even though she tried to turn her head away, and this time he didn't bother with any punishment but got straight down to the enjoyment, holding her against him until she was painfully aware of his arousal—and her own.

'If I didn't want you for another job entirely, I wouldn't wait another second for payment, Charley!' he said quietly, looking down at her. 'You've been wasted in that office. This is what you're intended for. You could build a whole new life around this. I never suspected that the smart suit covered so much pleasure.'

She was just lying there in his arms, leaning against him, her eyes wide and grey, staring into his as he raised his eyes from their moody contemplation of her lips.

'I admit to wanting you, Charley!' he said with a touch of self-contempt, 'but I'm not about to let it spoil my plans!'

'What—what plans?' she asked dazedly, aware only distantly that she was still held against a demanding, masculine body, that his hands were restless with desire and only his hard mind kept her safe from instant possession. Certainly she could not have helped herself, there were too many feelings raging inside her.

'I'll tell you later! When I'm good and ready,' he ground out, pulling her back to him, his mouth hotly on her skin and then determinedly on her own. 'For now, I'll take an advance payment this way!'

She was trembling all over when he finally let her go, and she could see that he was angry with himself and with her. His lips had been reluctant to leave hers, and even at the last second his hands had lingered on her. Whatever his plans were, they were certainly not this, and she supposed she should have been greatly relieved at that. He looked as if the enjoyment he got out of kissing her and touching her was a great and unacceptable surprise to him.

And he did enjoy kissing her! She looked at his tight shoulders as he walked to the window and looked out as she attempted to straighten her dress and come back to normality. He had admitted to wanting her, and it had surprised him. He hadn't needed to tell her. She had felt his hard, lean body surge against her own. She was not *that* innocent.

'I've had two or three meetings during this week,' he grated without turning. 'I couldn't take you with me and I know that you're safe here, coffee lounge lizards excluded.'

'I—I can deal with people perfectly well!' Charlotte said quickly, getting her bearings in a confused world that even now seemed to be swinging around her hazily. She got one of his sharp, hard laughs.

'Don't bank on it, Charlotte! You can't deal with me, for a start! Anyway,' he added irritably, 'if I see him hanging around you again, I'll deal with him!' He suddenly changed the subject in a bewildering manner. 'There's a reception tonight, quite important. Wear the green dress.'

'The turquoise one?' she corrected mildly, her face still flushed and bewildered.

'If you say so,' he grunted, pacing away from the window in a disgruntled manner, coming to stand in front of her. He looked at her silently for a second and then turned away.

'Get the hell out of here, Charley, before I change my mind!' he suddenly snapped.

She fled as quickly as possible, telling herself that she was not at all trapped, that she could walk out of this hotel and away from Kit Landor, but the thought of her uncle safe and secure across the Atlantic, well out of the reach of any thugs, and the thought of those same thugs waiting for her at home, gave her pause for thought. Next time he touched her she would . . . Would what? Sink into his arms? Behave like a weak and submissive idiot? She had always thrown books down in disgust if they contained women like that, and here she was still feeling those hard, lean hands possessively on her. And he was annoyed with himself! He was not the only one! She had a good line in self-condemnation at the moment!

CHAPTER FOUR

CHARLOTTE had to admit that the dress was beautiful, and that to attend a reception as a personal assistant to an important envoy from the American head office was definitely better than going to work in her smart suits to face Mrs Atkinson.

The dress showed off her youth and beauty, the clear turquoise chiffon swirling around her as she moved. She gave a few practice swirls in front of the morror in her bedroom, and felt quite light-headed at the effect; it hardly looked like her at all. Her thick, shining brown hair was brushed to one side and fastened back with a diamanté clasp that had been her mother's, and the off-the-shoulder style of the dress really made the best of her figure. She felt as if she was walking on air, until Kit tapped on her door and she saw him in a white dinner-jacket and black trousers, his face even more hard-looking than usual when he saw how she looked.

For a brief second, disappointment washed over her. Her face flushed as she discovered that she had wanted him to admire her appearance, that the 'walking on air' feeling had been partly anticipation. It made her deeply ashamed and her face clouded, the shame adding to her blushes.

'You would have preferred a different escort, Miss Roberts?' he said caustically. 'Sorry, you're stuck with me!'

'I just realised that as I saw you!' she managed pertly. 'How well you read my mind!'

'Not nearly so well as I read your body!' he growled, taking her arm impatiently. 'And as you're not exactly one of the ugly sisters, watch your step tonight—remember that you're with me. Keep your eyes on your escort!'

'I'll do that!' she snapped, as angry with herself as she was with him. 'I'm your personal assistant, after all!'

'A temporary inconvenience, I assure you!'

What did he mean by that? Was he sending her back to face the music because he had suddenly discovered that he—he wanted her? She didn't even like to *think* the phrase!

'That's better!' he commented in a satisfied voice as her anger changed to unease. 'The blushing, bewildered look goes with the dress. You need a nice, hard-looking suit to match that other look, and you're certainly no longer Miss Prim!'

'I'm really glad you think so!' Charlotte said tartly. 'You have no idea, thought, how I feel inside!'

'I know how you'll feel inside before this evening is over!' he snapped, marching her to the lift. 'I'll settle for that!'

It was not an auspicious beginning to the evening, but Charlotte's chin came up proudly. There was, after all, little left that he could shock her with—apart from . . . from . . . She refused to think about it!

They had moved into an even more luxurious part of the hotel, and her heart became a little unsteady at the glitter of the place that was clearly set aside for functions of this sort. There were plenty of pre-dinner drinks in the anteroom, but Charlotte was not used to drinking at all and made her one sherry last as long as possible, feeling that she had better keep her wits about her. She was very impressed to be in such a cosmopolitan gathering, beginning to recognise her own shortcomings as a

PA. She was completely out of her depth, and she felt that Kit must surely know it. He was used to this.

Kit kept her close to him at all times, and in spite of her annoyance with him she was very glad. There were no young people here, but there were a lot of very rich people, and all of them seemed to know Kit, no doubt because he represented Sanford Petrochemicals all over the world as their accountant.

The ladies were mostly middle-aged, and it did not take her long to realise that quite a few of them were more than interested in Kit. Of course, he was a very handsome man, in spite of his forbidding air of power and his aura of toughness. She was glad she had spent so much on the dress, realising now that she had really needed it.

She was simply introduced as Charlotte Roberts, nothing more, not 'my personal assistant' or 'part of the firm'. They probably thought she was just his friend, and the way he kept her tightly to his side gave her the impression that she was some sort of a shield against these beautiful but slightly predatory women. They all had escorts of their own, mostly husbands, she assumed, and it would not be to Kit's advantage to be seen talking too intimately with any one of them. This was probably her role, why he had wanted her here! The idea seemed more real every time she looked at it, and by the time that dinner began she was filled with a feeling of power herself, vengeance on her mind.

The dining-table was immense, shaped like a horseshoe, decked with flowers and silver, and Charlotte swept in to dinner on Kit's arm, amused to feel his eyes on her in a thoughtful way. At least, she thought they were, but when she glanced at him he was smiling to himself, an unheard-of thing! It worried her for a few minutes, but she returned to her thoughts of vengeance and soon had her opportunity.

The woman next to Charlotte was about thirty-five, very beautiful, not just pretty, her escort some sort of Middle Eastern prince by the look of him, and Charlotte was at first made rather uncomfortable by the fact that the lady in question spent a good deal of her time leaning across to speak to Kit.

She didn't mind being ignored, it suited her well, especially when she saw the husband in question give Kit a very grim look indeed. She smiled and left them to it, ignoring Kit's attempts to free himself of this excessive attention.

It was a little off-putting that the woman couldn't seem to make her mind up whether she was leaning across Charlotte from the front or from round her back. It necessitated a great deal of mobility on Charlotte's part, swinging forward and backward to allow the conversation to continue, trying really hard to look nonchalant while watching the husband's growing annoyance with inner glee. Kit, too, looked ready to strangle her, but had to keep on being affable. Oddly enough, that fact annoyed her. He was rarely affable with *her*!

'Your soup, madam.' The waiter succeeded at last in settling the woman for a moment as he served her soup, a gloriously colourful concoction that he ladled into her plate. She sat back and ignored him, although Charlotte's eyes were wide with wonder at this tropical-looking dish.

'Madam?' He bent over Charlotte just as the talkative lady darted forward again to Kit and, by now fairly trained to the movement, Charlotte darted back, straight into the waiter's arm!

The soup ladle rose vertically, but the soup fell in a bright stream of colour, quite fascinating to see, and the beautiful shoulders of the woman were suddenly covered with soup.

'Oh! I'm so sorry!' Her cool detachment deserting her, Charlotte sprang up, and the contents of the tureen, now held in hands that were not quite so dexterous, flooded over her own lovely turquoise dress as the waiter completely lost his balance at her unexpected and sudden movement.

There was silence, and then the woman's English deserted her as she reverted to a language that Charlotte did not know. The gist of it was clear however, and Charlotte already knew that she was clumsy, stupid, uneducated, and gauche. Kit looked astonished and Charlotte was filled with fury at him.

She was too angry to be embarrassed at the sight she looked as she marched out through the foyer of the hotel and got her bearings. All she thought of was getting to her room and closing the door behind her, trying to salvage something of this beautiful dress. She had given Kit no chance to assist her. She blamed him roundly for all of this.

Her first act was to race into her bathroom and take off the dress. The soup was so colourful that she knew it would make a permanent stain. The dress was ruined, and she had not even had one evening's wear out of it. She ran the bath, filling it with cold water, and sank the lovely dress into it.

As she showered, a slow rage filled her. So much for her vengeance! As usual, Kit Landor had got away untinged. The husband was murmuring comforting words to the woman as Charlotte had left. There had been no comfort murmured to *her*, and she was supposed to be with Kit!

That thought finally sank in as she stepped from the shower that Kit would send her back to face the music alone at the cottage, and it made her realise her stupidity in not going along quietly with him. He held every card.

No, he did not! She could simply leave here tomorrow and find a job elsewhere, send for her things.

She dried her hair and slipped into her nightie, a feeling of freedom inside her mixed with another feeling—regret that she would never see Kit again after she had walked off. She wouldn't even see him at all tomorrow, because she would be away before he came to collect her from breakfast. She sighed. It was a good thing, after all. She was getting just a little too used to the way he reached out and pulled her to him like a slave.

'Charlotte!' She stiffened and then slipped into her dressing-gown, ignoring his hard voice and the equally hard sound of his sharp rap on the door of her room.

'Charlotte! Open the door!'

She ignored him, knowing that he would become impatient and go. She had decided to disappear for a while. She was not about to be visible tonight.

She heard him go and relaxed a little, her heartbeats now reduced to normal, but her heart took on the unnatural hammering again as she heard the sound of voices outside her door and the sound of a key in the lock.

'Thanks! I expect she's all right but I think I'll just make sure!'

'No trouble, sir. Call the desk if the young lady is still not well.'

There was the sound of departing footsteps and then the closing of her door as Kit stepped into the room and shut out the rest of the secure world.

'What the hell are you up to?'

His glance flashed over her state of dress and her defiant face, apparently missing the uneasiness there. He sounded so annoyed that she stayed right where she was in the middle of the room, not even moving as he glanced around and then walked to the bathroom, his startled exclamation telling her that he saw the dress in the water.

'What the blazes are you doing with this?'

'It's a sure-fire way of removing stains!' she got out a little breathlessly, feeling less defiant and more shaky now that he was here and so annoyed. She hadn't realised that Americans could be so alien.

'It's a sure-fire way of getting shaken to death!' he rasped. Instead of suffocating her with a pillow, he strode to the phone an dialled reception.

'Send a maid up, please, at once!' he ordered curtly, and then he just stood quite still, no doubt waiting for her to apologise. She didn't!

She sat at the dressing-table and brushed her hair with as casual an air as she could manage, while the maid rinsed out the dripping dress and took it away. She could hear Kit speaking to her, explaining this débâcle, but he didn't often take his eyes away from Charlotte.

As the maid left and closed the door, though, he put an end to any further nonsense.

'Now, Miss Roberts!' He switched on the main lights. 'Let's have an explanation of this astonishing conduct!'

It wasn't possible to avoid him any more, so she faced him, too annoyed to be alarmed.

'It was an accident! You surely could see that. If your lady friend had kept still, none of it would have happened!'

'And if you hadn't been so damned accommodating to her we would by now be eating a civilised meal!' he shot back at her. 'Why didn't you change and come back down? You bought more than one dress!'

'I didn't choose to come back down!' she said angrily, her temper wild and her tongue unguarded. 'Tomorrow, I get a train out of London and you're on your own, Mr Landor!'

'I see.'

His quiet acceptance of this worried her more than an angry scene, but she stood her ground determinedly, even when he went to the phone and ordered dinner for two in her room.

'If you think that I'll . . .' she began angrily, but he shot her a look of cool enquiry, his dark eyebrows raised questioningly.

'You'll what, Charlotte?' he asked with a sinister softness. 'You'll shut up and you'll eat here with me. Furthermore, you'll eat exactly as you are, in that robe. I think it's about time that you were told what I want and *why* I'm going to get it!'

As usual, the cold blue eyes hypnotised her, and Charlotte found herself sitting in her robe, at a table prepared by the window, an intrigued waiter mindful of his manners but clearly fascinated by the well-dressed man and the girl in her nightwear. It embarrassed Charlotte almost to the edge of tears, certainly to the edge of blue murder, and her eyes were as narrowed and sparkling with anger as Kit's were narrowed and cool when the waiter eventually withdrew with a quickly speculative glance at her.

Kit settled her in her chair with a hostile look that was all-encompassing. He had clearly noted her angry face and it just about matched his own.

'This evening you were supposed to sit by me, talk to me and have eyes for nobody else but me!' he rasped as he sat opposite. 'It was your job! You produced an embarrassing fiasco!'

'I intended . . .'

'Don't bother!' he cut in irascibly. 'I recognise malice when I see it! Considering the trouble you're in, I would have thought that a slight curb on that temper would have been a good idea! More often than not you behave like a tearaway instead of a responsible adult!'

'I hardly think that you can chastise me on that score!' Charlotte said heatedly. 'You're certainly not a gentleman!'

'I've never attempted that unlikely feat!' he snapped. 'Let's get down to your problems!'

'I don't have any!' Charlotte said smugly. 'I ran in panic, I'll simply disappear discreetly until all this blows over. I do have friends! Somebody will collect my things, and I don't care if the Mafia are surrounding Lilac Cottage. Obviously it doesn't belong to us any more! They can't get Uncle Joe, as he's in America, and they'll not even look for me!'

'So! You figure that you're free and running wild?' he asked softly, with a look about him that she didn't like. She didn't like his expression either, or the way her eyes had begun to watch his lean fingers, his bronzed face.

'*I* don't really have any problems,' she said sharply. 'I'm an innocent bystander. Why I've put up with . . .'

'You have one big problem, Miss Roberts!' he said cynically. 'Your problem is called Joe!'

'What do you mean?' She could hear the anxiety in her voice, and so could he. He leaned back, glass in hand, and she found herself at the receiving end of that cold blue-eyed look that always alarmed her.

'Finish your meal,' he said softly, 'and I'll tell you a bedtime story.'

'I—I'm not hungry,' she stammered, all her defiance gone. He noted it with cold amusement.

'Did you know that your uncle started as a geologist?' he asked pleasantly, his own fork back in his hand, his eyes glancing up enquiringly as she shook her head. 'Well, he did! Since then, he's done about everything there is to do around an oilfield. I expect he knows the business better than almost anybody alive, apart from

Brett Sanford. In fact, he and Brett worked together for years before Brett took over the firm. He taught Joe just about everything he knows.'

Charlotte was stunned! She had no idea that her uncle had been so good at his job, that he knew Brett Sanford, the hard-headed chairman in Huston. No wonder they had let him go back! It was a great relief to hear it.

'This is supposed to worry me?' she asked sarcastically. 'Obviously you needed him!'

'Oh, we needed him!' Kit bit out. 'I haven't got to the interesting part yet, Charlotte!' He noted with satisfaction the unease back in her eyes before he went on, 'A gambler, a compulsive gambler, carries on wherever he is, whatever he's doing. Time after time, the firm has pulled him out of trouble, until this last time. It's not good image-making material for a firm as big as ours when "heavies" are hanging around, waiting to take the field manager apart, and that's what happened with Joe. Everything he had coming from the firm went to pay off his debts, and the firm got rid of him at once.'

He leaned back and watched her with a condemnation in his face, as if she was the cause of this, and Charlotte didn't have the nerve to make any comment; she knew her uncle was a compulsive gambler, he had said as much to her.

'A few weeks later,' he continued coldly, 'we moved in a new accounting team, and a few weeks after that, they called me. The debts that had taken Joe Roberts' compensation were the tip of the iceberg. He had been defrauding the company for months and months, thousands of dollars! Anybody who supplied equipment was paying through the nose for the privilege, and Joe had the rake-off! Mafia? He's a whole band of crooks rolled into one guy!'

'You're lying!' Charlotte snapped. Being a gambler didn't make her uncle into a crook. 'Hundreds of people gamble; it doesn't necessarily mean that they're dishonest! I don't know what you're up to, but if you think that . . .'

'I go to the races myself,' Kit said irascibly. 'Maybe it makes me into a gambler? Is that what you're suggesting? I use my own money, though, not the firm's!'

'My uncle Joe wouldn't——' Charlotte raged, quite beside herself at this new insult, but he cut in ruthlessly.

'Listen, Miss Prim and Proper,' he grated, 'compulsive gambling is not having a small wager on a horse, it's not having a merry flutter on some game of chance. A gambler of your uncle's type is sick, it's a disease! He thinks of nothing else! Your precious Joe would gamble on two flies going up a wall! It's a miracle that you've had a roof over your head this long. Men spend everything on gambling—money for their children's food, everything! It's a good indication of his affection for you that his misdeeds have only just hit you personally!'

'I can't believe . . .' Charlotte began, still infuriated, but the truth beginning to sink in horribly.

'Believe!' he snapped. 'He'll gamble with anything to hand, even if it's not his. He never imagines that it's dishonest, because he's always going to win! They all expect to win! They take more to put back what they lost, and gamble that to win, but they *lose*!'

The thought of the mortgage, the way he had admitted taking that money to try to win more instead of paying off his debts, silenced Charlotte. She believed it!

'Is—is that why—why you came to England?' Charlotte asked into the angry silence as the penny dropped loudly and painfully. She was so ashamed, not blaming Kit at all for the disgusted way he looked at her.

Her own conduct had been a bit odd, and right at this moment she wondered why he hadn't strangled her instead of kissing her. No wonder he had seemed angry as he held her! It was probably all his responsibility.

'Sure!' he said caustically. 'I came after Joe! When I saw you at the accident, I was on my way to the post office to track down your uncle. Joe was always a bit vague as to where he lived exactly in this country. I'd got this far. I was after the correct address. That's why I was driving away from the offices instead of towards them!'

And how quickly he had reacted when she had said that, Charlotte thought with horror. He was too clever by half. Another horrifying thought came to her.

'You got the address from me in the canteen!' she said numbly.

'Right!' he agreed with cold satisfaction. 'After that I decided to bide my time. There's no way we could get at Joe here in this country, but I wanted him real bad! Since he left I've had a lot of fast talking to do to keep the firm's reputation with the suppliers. I've had a lot of cheques to sign too, big cheques! When Joe does something, he does it well!'

'So that's why you—you took me out to lunch so often?' Charlotte said, watching him in wide-eyed shock as the whole picture slowly took shape. 'You—you were just b-biding your time!'

'Clever little Charley!' he sneered.

'I fell right into the trap, didn't I?' she asked miserably. 'Running to you as a friend.'

He just nodded tauntingly, his eyes narrowed on her stricken face.

'I was beginning to think it was just a waste of time,' he admitted with a humourless smile. 'You were so cagey, as if it was you who had something to hide, but I decided against that—you're not *that* smart! I could see that you didn't like me, though, and that you were waiting to see the back of me. I'd just about decided to go and see him when you came running for help!'

'Right into the trap!' Charlotte said unhappily. 'Now you've tricked him into going back. Will he go to prison?'

'Company dishonesty is viewed very severely in the States,' he said grimly. 'If we decide to prosecute, then he'll be in prison for a good while.'

'You—you mean . . . you might not prosecute?'

Charlotte's face was a picture of bewilderment and hope, and he watched her for a minute without speaking, then he said flatly, 'That's entirely up to you!'

'Me? Why me? What do you . . .'

'I need a wife, on a purely temporary basis,' he said abruptly. 'I want somebody who is completely under my thumb, who will jump when I say jump, and who can be got rid of when the job's done with no messy grief and wailing. I need a friendly wife, a wife who will pick up her big, fat cheque when the deal's over and disappear quietly. You marry me, Charlotte, or Uncle Joe pays the price of dishonesty!'

'You—you're quite mad!' Charlotte gave him a horrified look that only added to his normal irritation. 'In any case,' she added quickly, 'you don't have the authority to keep Uncle Joe out of prison! What's decided will not be up to you. He—he's probably in prison right now!' she finished in a subdued voice, tears beginning to sparkle in her eyes.

'I have and he's not!' Kit said briefly, adding, 'I'm the chief accountant for a giant firm. I swing a lot of weight. Anyway, I've stashed Joe in the Alaskan field, and I'm the only one who knows it. He's safe so long as I get what I want!'

'Why are you doing this?' Charlotte whispered. 'Why

don't you just fall in love and get married like—like everybody else does?'

He gave a harsh bark of laughter.

'Love?' he jeered. 'Charlotte! I'm thirty-five and I've never run into that mythical state yet! It doesn't happen!'

'It does!' Charlotte said heatedly, annoyed at his cynicism. 'People are doing it all the time! You'll have to join the ranks, because I'm not marrying you!'

'Goodbye, Joe!' he said softly. 'It's a long way to the States for visiting days!' He suddenly shot her an exasperated look. 'Stop talking nonsense, Charlotte! I can do without this "up in the air" talk that women indulge in! How old are you? Twenty-two, twenty-three? You've never been in love in your short and busy life!'

'Well, you're wrong there!' she said triumphantly, hating his scathing voice.

'Who was he?' he demanded, so obviously sceptical.

'He's not dead, so don't speak of him in the past!' she said with an edge to her voice. 'He's called Gordon and he lives in—in the town!'

'So why wasn't he standing right beside you and Joe, manning the barricades?' he asked coldly, disbelief written all over his face. 'Why run to me instead of Gordon?' He said the name as if it was very soiled, and she had a sudden picture of Gordon standing steadfastly beside her in trouble. It didn't ring true.

'Why the hell didn't he marry you?' he continued irritably. 'What's he waiting for?'

'Another girl, I expect!' she snapped. 'I stopped going out with him. I stopped being in love!'

'Which goes to prove my point,' he said, quietly satisfied. 'All this life-long devotion is a myth. Why?' he suddenly shot at her.

'Why what? Why did I stop being in love? I don't know! I stopped seeing him because . . .' She suddenly blushed fiercely, remembering exactly why she had stopped seeing Gordon. It wasn't that which brought the blushes, though it was the realisation that Kit Landor had already held her closer, touched her more intimately than Gordon had attempted. And for those attempts, he had got his marching orders.

'How long were you in love with this jerk?' he asked softly, recognising her dismay, as if he knew exactly what she was thinking.

'A-about six months,' Charlotte said hastily, her eyes avoiding his.

'That's about par for the course!' he assured her ironically. 'Putting Gordon aside,' he added with a dry look at her flushed face, 'my motives are strictly for friendship. I want to get a married woman out of my hair, and to be married myself will do the trick nicely.'

'Why don't you tell her to drop dead?' Charlotte said resentfully, suddenly not liking the idea of anyone, married or otherwise, in Kit's arms. The knowledge that she resented it only added to her sharpness, and he glanced at her reprovingly.

'Her husband is a friend, my best friend!' he snapped. 'She married him, not me, but she can't seem to get the idea fixed in her head. I don't want a break with him and I want rid of her.'

'How long will it take?' she asked reasonably.

'A year, maybe less, maybe more.' His eyes narrowed again at her sensible tone. 'You can then walk off with a nice bonus, plenty of clothes . . .'

'You're rich then, are you?' Charlotte asked interestedly. 'You have more than the expense account?'

'Enough to satisfy you!' he bit out, watching her closely.

'You couldn't satisfy me if you were the last man in the universe!' Charlotte ground out loudly, standing and looking down at him in a queenly manner, her head proudly held. 'How you dare put such an idea to me is utterly outside my experience!'

'Just about everything is outside your experience!' he said, only amused at her attitude, not believing it at all. 'What about poor Joe?'

'You can go and——'

She never got any further. He was on his feet instantly, rounding the table and grasping her with steely hands.

'Let's go together, shall we?' he muttered angrily as his lips ground into hers.

It was like free-falling from a plane, rocketing in the air, drowning! The minute his lips touched hers he cunningly changed his mind and began to kiss her druggingly, slowly and with obvious pleasure. She felt quite fatalistic as he parted the lapels of her robe, his hand moving inside to slip beneath the lace top of her nightie and search for her breast. She could feel the anger in him as his body surged against hers, his arousal instantaneous, and the hard hand that fondled her breast was not gentle.

Even so, she felt a shameful delight in it, shafts of pleasure piercing her whole body.

'I could get to hate you, Charley!' he murmured against her mouth, his lips hardly lifting. 'You do this on purpose! You're certainly not as innocent as I thought!'

He suddenly pushed her away so roughly that she almost overbalanced, her eyes still glazed with the hard passion that had seared from him.

'You'll marry me, or Joe gets exactly what he's been asking for for years!' he grated.

She found that memories of her Uncle Joe's goodness to her, to her mother, the way he had taken them in when her father died, the way he had supported her for years, began to swamp even the wild feelings that Kit had forced into her. He must love her very much to have controlled his gambling until now. She couldn't let him go to prison. Why not have a temporary marriage with Kit? It was only a job, after all. A job like any other. Unusual, perhaps, but then, what choice did she have?

'I'll not . . . If you expect me to . . .' She left off, flustered, and he looked at her with a hard triumph on his face.

'Sleep in my bed?' he enquired insultingly. 'You should be so lucky! I'm never short of that sort of friend—they queue up! If you want your share, you'll have to wait until your number comes up!'

She could imagine! He had got that expertise from somewhere!

'Thank you!' she said in a dignified voice. 'I'll take the job without the perks.'

Suddenly he laughed, that brilliant burst of laughter that could sometimes light up his whole face, making him irresistible, and to her dismay Charlotte felt her heart leap in her chest.

'We'll discuss your new duties tomorrow,' he said with amusement in his blue eyes. 'I think I'd better go now, while I'm still partially in control of my own mad inclinations. Goodnight, Miss Prim!'

She was still shivering and flushed when the waiter came for the remains of the meal, and he looked at her closely before glancing round to see where Kit was. Obviously he thought the man was mad, unless he imagined that Kit had hidden under the bed. Charlotte gave him one of her stern, old-fashioned looks, and he left, greatly puzzled.

CHAPTER FIVE

HER fate decided, Kit cancelled all his other appointments and they went back to the cottage, Charlotte in a completely different frame of mind from the way she had felt when they had left it just under a week ago. Since she had agreed to his plans, Kit had left her severely alone, and she knew that his attention to her before had been merely part of the trickery. If his threats had failed he would have been quite prepared to enslave her and talk of marriage on a temporary basis. He had picked her out because she was vulnerable and in trouble. He was ruthless, utterly unfeeling, and he now treated her like an employee, a very lowly one.

Initially, he left her at the cottage and disappeared, his parting words making her feel still more lonely.

'I'll go to the office and let them know you won't be coming back.'

'Are you going to tell them that—that . . .'

'Naturally not!' he bit out, not even giving her time to finish. 'The marriage will be over before they get wind of it. Why tell the world?'

'Then—then I'll be able to come back here to work,' Charlotte said hopefully. He scotched that plan.

'No! It wouldn't be suitable, not after you've been married to me! When the time comes I'll find another firm to employ you.'

That really put her in her place, made her feel inadequate for the first time in her life. He was quite prepared apparently to drive off and leave her here alone, the trouble that could ensue not entering his mind. She hated now to ask for help, but she had to.

'How long will you be?' she asked a little anxiously, and his hard glance assured her that he would not be telling her of his whereabouts for the duration of any marriage.

'You have a reason to want me back soon?' he asked scathingly.

'It—it's the men!' she said shortly, her face flushing at his obvious innuendo.

'Forget the men!' he rasped, dismissing the whole affair as if it had been no problem. 'From the morning that Joe took off, there have been no men. I paid that debt. I arranged it the night before and paid it off before I ever came in for my breakfast. So there is not and never has been a mob chasing you!'

'Uncle Joe agreed to—to that?' she gasped, her legs folding under her as she desperately searched for a seat and sank into it.'

'The choice wasn't his!' Kit said bitingly. 'We have offices in this town. The name of Sanford is the most important thing in my life. We've had enough mobsters around, thanks to Joe Roberts, and I wasn't about to have any exciting news in the papers about one of our employees having to skip the country to get away from them! Joe's had the sharp edge of my tongue around him more than once. I didn't ask his opinion! He does as he's told, like you!'

It hurt! It actually hurt and that made her angry.

'If I'd known about that,' Charlotte snapped, 'I could have stayed and worked! I still can! I may be afraid of a gang of ruffians, but I'm not afraid of work. I could finally pay you back. If I can manage to keep the cottage I can . . .'

'The cottage is yours!' Kit cut in briskly. 'I fixed

that, too!'

'You paid off that mortgage? All that money?'

'Hell! I'm rolling in money! The cottage is now in your name. If all this bothers you then we'll call it a wedding present, but it's all over and done with and I don't want to hear about it again! As to staying and working instead of marrying me, aren't you forgetting something? Joe's right in my hand and teetering on the edge of a long spell in jail. That's why you're marrying me, and that's why you'll do exactly as you're told.'

'You callous, deceitful, cold-hearted brute!' Charlotte sprang to her feet, her hands clenched together, and he looked at her with an air of menace that she didn't at first notice in her anger.

'Callous? I pull you out of every scrape there is, and I'm callous?' he demanded with a very deceptive quiet.

'You did it to trick me into marrying you! That's callous! I feel as if I've been bought! I feel cheap!'

He lunged forward and grasped her wrist, pulling her to him with a quick and angry twist of his arm.

'Do you?' he snapped. 'What's cheap, after all? To my way of thinking, your precious Uncle Joe is pretty cheap! *He* landed you in this hole, not me! I was just looking for somebody to get rid of Veronica without breaking up a long and valued friendship. You are cancelling out all Joe's debts by simply doing a job, however distasteful you find me! I sure hope he realises what a sacrifice you're making for him!' he snarled. 'My heart bleeds for you! Maybe I'd better end all this farce now and drop Joe into the nearest jail!'

'No! No, I'm sorry!' Charlotte's face went utterly white at the thought. Kit was so furious that he looked

capable of storming out of here and leaving her to her
fate while he pursued her uncle. He had also made her
feel somewhere in the region of one inch high. He had
gone to enormous expense to leave everything
perfectly normal and unblemished in her home town;
nobody would know about her uncle's shame or her
own. Shame was what she felt now. Kit looked at her
as if she was tarnished, tarred with the same brush as
her uncle. She owed him too much to let him down,
and right now she felt incapable of saying anything in
her own defence at all.

'So, I'm a heel!' he said with a peculiar tightness to
his voice, a good deal of the anger leaving him. 'I've
tricked you, bought you, whatever your idiotic mind
wants to make it. Well, I'm not sorry, so don't go
expecting any apologies! I need you and I'm keeping
you for as long as I require your services! You'll fool
Veronica with no problem, she's not too bright! I
don't want a normal marriage. I can do without a
woman clinging to my neck whenever things don't
suit her. I like freedom and I'm going to go right on
keeping my freedom! You can count me as a friend
whenever you need one, but just get off my back! Stop
yelling at me and trying to excuse everybody else! I
know my crimes, they can be stretched from here to
New York, no doubt, but right at the moment we're
concerned with Joe's crimes and your new job! That's
all it's going to be, Charlotte, a job!'

'All right!' she said shakily. 'I'll do my best. Just
don't—don't touch me, that's all.' She pulled her wrist
away from his hard grasp, rubbing it where his fingers
had sunk into her tender skin.

His eyes narrowed as he looked down at her.

'Then don't push your luck!' he growled. 'Just
remember that I'm a perfectly normal male, and you,

Charlotte, are very young and very beautiful. Any touching will be a necessity, to assist in your role as my wife, all done in public. Don't make the mistake of stepping in my path, though. I go my own way, and if I'm hassled you'll pay—in the best way possible—for me!'

She was shaking like a leaf, her own anger gone at his tirade of savage words, the cottage suddenly very empty and lonely around them, and he grimaced wryly, pulling her into his arms, that soothing hand on the back of her neck.

'Calm down,' he said more softly. 'In a couple of days we've got to face people as we get married. Angry words are the last thing we want, because it will show for a good while, especially with your expressive face. For now, we've got to look as if we're crazy about each other.'

'You're going to have a hard job there,' she mumbled against his chest, every bit of tension leaving her as soon as he was in any way gentle again. 'Your opinion of love shows.'

'Just don't bother about me, Charley!' he said drily, pushing her away and walking to the door. 'I'm a first-rate liar. You're the one with the acting problem.'

She watched his broad back, his easy swinging walk as he went to his car, and dismay flooded through her. For a moment she had felt safe, comfortable, and the frightening beginnings of a clamour deep inside that had vanquished her anger. The trouble that her uncle had brought on her was nothing to the trouble that she was beginning to suspect she had as far as Kit was concerned. To fall in love with him would be madness of the worst kind, but she was begining to feel waves of enchantment when he was near that she had never felt before. If he even suspected, he would play on it for all it was worth. Her acting ability had better improve smartly!

He simply drove off, leaving her there to pack her possessions, not one worry in his head about her, and she wandered disconsolately around the cottage. It was hard to believe it possible now she was back in her own home town that she was in such a fix.

The days since she had come home to find her uncle almost paralysed with fear seemed to have been a complete dream but, after Kit had gone, the realisation that it was true struck home deeply. She was allowing herself to be bullied and frightened into a marriage that was as frightening as the original shock her uncle had dealt her. Now that he was alone, she admitted it.

There were the things that belonged to them, furniture, clothes, the innumerable small object that one accumulated during a lifetime of living in one place, and everything had to be packed. Better sooner than later! She started packing things up, sorting out her uncle's things and hers into two separate groups, but she was bitter and lonely and filled with a growing fear of the future as Kit's wife, no matter how temporary the arrangement was. Even now, she longed for the sight of his tall, lithe frame, the sight of his determined and aloof face.

By the late afternoon she was sunk into total misery. He had not come back. He had told her that he only had a few things to collect from his flat and then he would be handing over the keys to the agent and returning for her. He had not, though, and she suddenly felt sure that he had changed his mind, some other plan had come to him. It was madness, but she found to her dismay that she missed him. They had been away only such a short time, and in that time this town was already nothing to do with her; she wanted to be where Kit was.

She told herself that it was his attitude, the way he organised things, leaving nothing to her. Kit had introduced her to a new life, even though she had only caught a glimpse of it, and there was more than that. She had spent a great deal of her teens being almost a mother to her Uncle Joe. She realised now how much he had relied on her for even the smallest things. She had stayed in to keep him company, taken all the responsibility for the house, even though she worked. It had left little time for anything else, not much time to be young.

Even the responsibility that Mrs Atkinson had placed on her slender shoulders at an early age had been tying, and now she looked at herself seriously and knew that she was not nearly as tough as she had imagined. If Kit found that out, he would soon see that she was unsuitable for his plans. When the chips were down, she had run to Kit. Worries clouded her mind, making her jumpy, and she got very little more done, not even bothering to switch on the lights as the day faded.

It was dusk when Kit came back, and he attacked immediately.

'Charlotte? What the hell are you doing in the dark? Why haven't you got the lights on?'

His softly harsh voice growled at her from the gloom of the outside as she opened the door, and she stared at him for a second, appalled that she wanted to rush forward to him, to feel those strong, hard arms wrapping her close.

'Kit! I—I thought you weren't coming back!'

'Sorry to disappoint you!' he remarked drily, walking into the darkened hall and switching on the lights.

He turned to her as she blinked in the sudden brightness. Her tiredness and her unhappiness were very plain to see as he stood looking down at her, his hands in his pockets, and after one swift glance at the brilliantly blue, narrowed eyes, she looked back at her own toes.

'How much packing have you done?' he asked impatiently.

'Not—not much. I started, but . . .'

She was embarrassed now because he didn't look too impressed with her at the moment, and she had to remind herself that if she became unsuitable then her uncle would go to prison. Kit had no reason to help when her usefulness ended.

'I suppose I'll have to sort you out!' he said testily, looking around to find out if anything at all had been done. 'Make some coffee!' he ordered, and she knew that the sorting out had begun.

His quick glance at his watch and his hard voice made her feel as if she had caused no end of additional complications by not moving like a whirlwind and finishing everything in one hour flat. Her temper threatened to surface, but he took one look at her growing mutiny and his look silenced any words that were on the tip of her tongue.

She gladly stayed in the kitchen as he got on the phone, the strangely familiar American accent drifting to her from time to time as he spoke first to one person and then to another.

'Right!' He strode back into the kitchen after a few minutes and sat on the edge of the table, looking down at her. 'First thing in the morning the men will be here to pack this lot! Your things can be crated and shipped straight off home to the States. Your uncle Joe's things can go into store. The furniture can be stored too, until you decide what pieces you want to take with you.'

'Oh! Will I be able to do that?' She looked up at him hopefully. Some of the furniture here was her mother's, and she had a great desire to take it with her, something of her own.

'You can now do anything you damned well want, Charlotte!' he said decisively. 'All you have to remember is that it's very temporary!'

'I wouldn't want it to be anything else!' she snapped, her eyes a little over-bright with the threat of tears at his harshness.

Apparently he had been more harsh than he had intended, because as her face clouded at his tone he stood and walked around to her, pulling her to her feet and into his arms.

'Don't look at me like that,' he said softly. 'I'm not going to bite you!' He tilted her chin and looked down at her. 'I'm not at all poor, Charley,' he assured her quietly. 'You can have pretty much anything that you want while you're with me, and I'll see to it that you're fixed up nicely afterwards.'

'I'd like to take my mother's furniture,' she admitted, her eyes a little wistful on his face. 'It would be nice to have things I know around me.'

'I'll have the whole cottage moved stone by stone if you like,' he assured her maddeningly, back to his sardonic ways.

'What I would like,' she said nastily, 'is for this to be a nightmare and to wake up realising that I'd never even seen you!'

He looked down at her witheringly, still holding on to her, and she suddenly realised she had made no attempt to pull away. When she tried it he merely tightened her to him.

'You don't really know me, Charley,' he warned with a quiet that was alarming. 'If you think back, you'll realise it was only few weeks ago that we first met.'

'You don't know me, either, for that matter,' she reminded him sharply, her face slowly flushing as he continued to stare at her. 'Maybe you're going to regret this.'

It was really tricky to try to sound threatening when he was hovering above her like Nemesis, and the idea of being married to him, having to face him day after day, was quite alarming to say the very least.

'Not me, Charley,' he told her quietly. 'I know exactly what I want.'

She just went on staring up at him, and he seemed quite content to stay as he was, holding her, meeting her clear gaze; and she knew that he could see the uncertainty in her eyes.

Her gaze was drawn to the firm lips even against her will, and his hands tightened on her.

'It's nice to know that you don't find me utterly repulsive,' he said softly as his head bent to hers.

By a supreme effort she twisted away and he let her go, watching her with amused eyes.

'Don't worry, Charley,' he mocked. 'That part of the preparation is over. I know now that you can act the part well, kiss me in public and look as if you mean it, wear beautiful clothes like a princess, look wistfully enchanting. You'll go down a bomb with Veronica. Now, let's get to a hotel for the night!'

His lips twisted derisively and she turned away in annoyance. Her annoyance, though, was mainly directed at herself, and there was no way that she was going to let him see that. She had *wanted* him to kiss her, only coming to her senses at the last minute, contrarily wanting him to insist when she had pulled aside. She must be going mad!

There were firms, he said, to deal with packing, and a firm duly arrived, not at all concerned that it was Saturday morning, glad of the chance to get the trade. The packing she had expected to take her days to do was done in a couple of hours, and all she had to do was hover about and give instructions. Kit stayed there firmly throughout the whole proceedings, bringing her from the hotel and then standing by like a very alert watchdog, not that she even thought of escape, after all. She was a hostage and he knew it.

Before they left the cottage, it was completely emptied, thing stored and things despatched to America with no trouble at all. The power of the dollar was dictating the pace.

They were married in London. Two of Kit's friends acted as witnesses and, although there was no white wedding, it was oddly beautiful in its own way. Charlotte wore a cream silk suit and a large picture hat, her glossy brown hair shining in the sunlight as they stepped out of the little church.

He had given her no time to be either afraid or to change her mind, and she realised now that she was securely trapped, her unusual job a secret that only she and Kit shared. He had also kept her well away from his friends until the actual wedding, so that she was completely surrounded by strangers at the ceremony and at the reception afterwards.

The wedding breakfast was in a very expensive London hotel, and Dora Crest, the wife of Kit's friend Gil, seemed to realise her nervousness.

'I know how you feel, Charlotte,' she said in a low voice as Kit and Gil talked to the other guests. 'It must be absolutely overwhelming to have to fly out to

America and face a life as Kit's wife after the quiet and peace of this country. It would be a shock in any case, but becoming a relative of Brett Sanford would have me shaking in my shoes!'

Everything in Charlotte came to attention, her mind chasing itself around as she tried to react normally to what she imagined she had just heard.

'I—I suppose that Kit will introduce me to his relatives in a while,' she said cautiously. 'There's no hurry.'

'No hurry?' Dora Crest almost exploded with laughter. 'Charlotte! Kit has married here, in England! He has no relatives except Brett Sanford, and if you think that Brett will take kindly to being kept away from the wedding of his only grandson, then think again! Brett will want to know exactly who this girl is who's going to be Mrs Landor and by Kit's side when Kit finally takes over Sanford Petrochemicals!'

It was probably the biggest shock that Charlotte had ever had in her life, and how she managed to shrug it off she never knew. Kit helped, of course. He turned at that moment and took one look at her face and was beside her instantly.

'Come over here, honey,' he said softly, his arm tightly around her waist. 'You're neglecting some of your guests!'

He never asked what was wrong, but he knew that something was, and Charlotte pulled out all the stops, smiling and talking, although she felt sick with shock and fright. Brett Sanford, the great American oil king, and he was Kit's grandfather! She knew now why Kit had said he was rolling in money—it was oil money! She felt utterly betrayed, and so lost that she hardly knew what she said any more.

Dora's final whisper as they left the hotel did nothing

to help, either.

'Just watch your step when you get into Kit's world. There are always women who flock around rich men, especially men so damned attractive as Kit Landor.' Charlotte had been left in no doubt about that by Kit himself. She already had that titbit of information!

They had already booked into a hotel the day before and deposited their luggage, and Charlotte kept silent until they were finally in the suite of rooms Kit had reserved. She had been going over in her mind the sheer enormity of it all, and she spun round to face him as the door closed behind them, a very wild aggression on her face.

'OK! Let's have it, all guns at once!' he bit out, tossing the keys on to the table and walking into the central sitting-room to turn and face her, his hands in his pockets. 'What did Dora tell you that had you near collapse?'

'You lied to me! Everything you've said has been a lie!' she accused angrily. 'You're the grandson of Brett Sanford! You said that you were an accountant for Sanford Petrochemicals. You *are* Sanford Petrochemicals!'

'So? What difference does that make?' he asked, narrow-eyed. 'You married me because your uncle is in deep trouble and I need a helping hand with a certain lady! Don't bother to talk as if I betrayed a great love! This is business, and who I am is *my* business!'

'You—you think I can manage to play your wife in—in the atmosphere of all that wealth?' Charlotte whispered, stricken beyond words at his callous answer. 'I'm ordinary! I can't cope with things like that. I had no idea what to expect beyond the fact that there was an unwelcome love affair to be got rid of! Now I'm expected to move in circles that are beyond my capabilities altogether, like—like *Dallas!*'

She was white as a sheet, her mind still reeling from shock, and he just stood there looking at her as if she was an unexpected oddity he had found in the room.

'Aren't you going to say anything?' she demanded frantically, wondering whether or not to simply run off and leave him to it.

'Sure!' he said softly. 'Pack your things, we're leaving now!'

'What?' Charlotte stared at him with wide, horrified eyes. 'We're going to America—*now?*'

'No!' He shook his head, his eyes still watching her in that odd, calm way. 'I wouldn't throw you in at the deep end without a rehearsal, Charlotte. We're going on honeymoon. Every newly-wed couple does it. It's expected.'

'When I first saw you,' Charlotte said unevenly, sitting down with no intention of moving, 'I thought you were strange. I now recognise my feelings as an instinctive alarm reaction, the mind's ability to alert one to danger. I recognised you as mad without even knowing it. You want a honeymoon? Then take one alone, because we have an agreement and it does not include a honeymoon!'

He was laughing again, that rare and wonderful laugh that could make her heart leap, and he came across and hauled her to her feet.

'Nothing sinister, Charley,' he assured her. 'All I intend is to get to know you, to let you get to know me. We're in this together, and when it's over you'll be very well paid. I can afford to make you wealthy, surely now you realise that?'

'I don't want to be wealthy!' Charlotte said desperately. 'I just want to go home!' she finished rather pitifully, and he gathered her tightly to him, looking down into her face.

'We're in this together,' he said firmly. 'If either of us makes a mistake, then I assure you, I'll be the one to suffer. As to going home, I intend to take you home, to *my* home. Just trust me a little, Charley!'

'How can I?' she murmured, further alarmed that she was not now so shaken when he held her, her worries simply draining away. 'You tell me lies all the time.'

'Pack your things!' he suddenly bit out impatiently. 'I've booked a honeymoon and we're taking it. It's going to be a talking honeymoon!'

He almost pushed her away and she knew why—she had been slowly melting towards him and that was the last thing he wanted, a clinging wife. She had more chance of delighting him if she aimed the occasional blow at his head!

He had booked them in at a small inn by the Thames, way out in the country, and Charlotte's tightly held in breath left her in a small sigh as she saw it. It was quiet, remote even, and maybe this time he was telling the truth.

'No problems!' he assured her, glancing at her as he stopped the car. 'Here we can spend a few days resting and talking. We can walk and really get to know each other. That way we'll be ready for anything when we get back home to the States!'

Charlotte forbore to mention that the States was not in any way her home, she even managed a smile, and his eyebrows raised sardonically.

'That's the first smile I've seen in days, apart from the rather glassy efforts you managed at the wedding!' he mocked. 'Lucky these folks here don't know that we're newly-weds. As it is, they'll think we're here to discuss a divorce!'

'I like the setting!' Charlotte said tartly. 'Can we come back when we're getting divorced? It will bring back such happy memories!'

Kit's lips twisted wryly, and she wished suddenly that she had held her tongue. She no longer wanted to annoy him. There was this very real feeling of a small amount of time, and she realised bitterly that she wanted it to last, whatever his sins might be.

It was low and oak-beamed inside, and Charlotte stood by Kit at the reception desk and read a long illuminated screed about the origins of this old inn as they waited for someone to come.

'Ah, yes, Mr and Mrs Landor!' the woman who finally came announced triumphantly. 'We've changed your rooms to the Honeymoon Suite!'

Charlotte stiffened instantly, her ease leaving her in a wild rush of embarrassment. Kit was not embarrassed, he was furious!

'Then could you just change back to the rooms I booked?' he said tightly.

'Oh, but Mr Landor, your friend, a Mr Crest, called last night and changed them. It's to be a surprise!'

'It is!' Kit bit out. 'My friend has a very warped sense of humour! You can leave it now, but tomorrow we want the rooms I booked, or I'm afraid we'll have to go elsewhere!'

It was all very embarrassing, although Kit apparently felt nothing but quiet rage.

'Why didn't you insist on changing now?' Charlotte hissed as they went upstairs behind the waiter who apparently doubled for everything else. 'Why do we have to endure even one night like this?'

'You'll see!' Kit said tightly. 'Gil has an even more warped sense of humour than I told the woman at the desk!'

It was a delightful room, and Charlotte would have been thrilled to have it, had it been for her alone. The bed was a four-poster, draped in white lace, the furniture old stripped pine, the en-suite bathroom the height of luxury, and on the round table by the window was a silver bucket with champagne all ready for them.

'Gil!' Kit assured her in a taut voice as she eyed the champagne and the large double bed. He threw his jacket off and walked towards the champagne determinedly. 'As he's paid for it, we may as well drink it!'

'Why are you being so casual about this?' Charlotte demanded angrily. 'You surely don't imagine that I'm sleeping in here with you?'

'I fail to see where you have much choice, unless we're to give the game away!' Kit said calmly, reaching for the glasses. 'In the morning there'll be a small knock on the door and breakfast will be served here at this table by the window. I'll be in my robe and you'll be in a very sweet négligé. The breakfast will have been ordered already by telephone, and in the middle of it Gil will waltz in with a few cronies to check on the state of our marriage!'

'You've got to be joking!' Charlotte said heatedly, her eyes on the bed that seemed to have lured her over to it. 'This is a double bed! Even if I felt like playing games for the benefit of your friends, there's no way I would sleep here!'

'Lower your voice!' Kit bit out quietly. 'I do not have the intention of broadcasting our affairs to the whole place! Gil is the chief accountant for Sanford Petrochemicals, and he knows Brett!'

'But you're the chief accountant!' Charlotte reminded him bitterly and loudly. 'You're also an accomplished liar, a cheat, a . . .'

'I said shut up!' he rasped, striding to her and grasping her arms. 'There's no need to get hysterical. We'll work something out!'

'You'll work yourself out of the door!' she snapped, louder than ever, and his patience snapped, too.

'If you can't stop, then I'll have to stop you!' he grated, his arms lashing round her.

This time, though, she was not about to melt. She was humiliated and angry, sure deep down that Kit had done this himself or arranged for Gil to do it. Her handbag was still in her hand and she used it as a weapon, aiming it carelessly but efficiently, not caring where the blows landed so long as they did, and Kit was even less amused than before.

'You little hell-cat!' he muttered, snatching the bag and tossing it across the room. 'Will you listen to reason?'

Charlotte didn't answer. She was so enraged at this insulting disregard for her intelligence that she simply took over with her hands as her handbag was removed.

He tripped her, and as she landed on the bed he came down on top of her, forcing her into the soft mattress and glaring into her eyes as he held her by the wrists.

'God! You're impossible!' he snarled. 'Some sweet wife you'll make!'

She opened her mouth to continue the battle, but he stopped that by crushing her lips with his, his mouth hard and punishing, his intention to subdue her as quickly and efficiently as possible. He was powerful, strong and heavy. His lips hurt, and the feeling of being trapped filled Charlotte with panic until she could hardly breath.

'Kit! Don't!' She tore her mouth away and he saw her eyes filled with fright and tears as he looked down at her with his cold blue gaze.

'Stop shouting, then' he ordered quietly. 'Stop fighting me and listen to reason!'

She nodded defeatedly and he moved slowly, his hard body brushing hers, his eyes intently on her face as her cheeks flushed rose-wild. Instead of rising, he rolled to the side and pulled her into her arms.

'I had no intention of being here, Charley,' he assured her quietly, his hand in her hair as he raised her face to meet his blue gaze. 'I had no intention of frightening you, either. Gil has done this, I promise you, and you have no idea how close the States are at this moment. There's a tightly welded pack of Americans in London who live in each other's pockets. They gossip like girls at school. They're all part of the firm and it all gets back to Brett one way or another. Believe me?' he asked softly.

Charlotte nodded, her fright ebbing now that she could move freely.

'I—I don't like being trapped,' she admitted tremulously, and he nodded slowly.

'I could see that in your eyes,' he assured her. 'So you see, we already know something about each other. If anyone ever traps you I'll know to lambast them right away!'

A smile touched Charlotte's lips, and his eyes echoed it at once, his hand soothing on her hot cheek; and when his head bent towards her she made no attempt to avoid him. He had promised that the rehearsals for this were over, but right now she wasn't counting at all. His lips took hers gently, and she told herself that lots of people kissed each other and it made no difference at all. People who hardly knew each other kissed, and she knew Kit very well.

Every excuse she could think of raced through her mind, but the main one was and always would be that she wanted him to kiss her. As the kiss deepened, her arms went around his neck as if they had made their own minds up, and Kit gathered her closer, his body half over hers, his hands beginning to caress her with growing urgency.

'You're quite crazy, Charley,' he murmured against her mouth. 'You know damned well I want you. You shouted and raved about something that is quite negotiable, but now when you should be fighting you're soft and warm, just asking for something you'll certainly get before long!'

She knew, but it was so wonderful, and for once he was gentle. Fright was a thing of the past, and she sighed against his lips as his hand undid the buttons of her dress and moved inside to capture her breast, his fingers expertly teasing, his touch delighting her.

He pressed more deeply over her, his lips moving slowly over her skin, along the column of her slender neck and down between the mounds of her breasts, to linger over the heavy beating of her heart. His caressing hands were becoming urgent, and he murmured against her skin, his voice taut.

'Fight, damn you, Charley!' he whispered harshly, but she was in a dream, completely spellbound, her voice little more than a sigh.

'I can't! You're so gentle!'

'Of course I am!' he rasped, tearing himself away and standing in one fluid movement. 'I'm seducing you!'

He pulled her to her feet, fastening the buttons of her dress and holding her in front of him, his eyes filled with anger.

'Look!' he said tightly, even giving her a little shake when she simply stared at him like someone in a trance. 'I want no involvement with you at all! You know why I married you and I know perfectly well that you dislike me intensely as a person, that you disapprove of almost every aspect of my life! I told you fair and square right off that I want you! It surprised me, irritated me and annoyed me, but it's there! It's not going to go away until I'm satisfied! Relax one inch, drop that fiery guard for one second, and I'll take you!'

The only thing fiery about Charlotte was her face, and he turned away abruptly, his shoulders tight and angry.

'Having proved to you what a dog I am,' he snapped, 'I'll now get us out of this mess! Tidy your hair and wait here!'

He strode from the room and slammed the door behind him, and Charlotte hastily began to follow his instructions, her eyes still a little dazed when a bewildered waiter, the same one, came back with Kit and took their luggage to the car.

'What are we going to do?' she asked worriedly as he drove angrily out on to the road.

'I've paid for the nights we were going to stay here!' he growled. 'When Gil bursts in tomorrow morning, and he *will*, he'll get the surprise of his life, especially as I've said they can let it and keep the money! We are going to another hotel miles away which we will choose at random! We'll also have two nice separate rooms! One night where we were, and you would most certainly not have been any longer the innocent Charlotte Roberts!'

'I'm Charlotte Landor now,' Charlotte reminded him quietly and bitterly.

'Landor or Roberts, it would have happened, and I would still have divorced you when the time came!' he said harshly. 'Bear that in mind next time you soften up!'

She would! It was like a slap, a reprimand; it made her feel cheap and soiled, and there were no smiles as they booked in to a hotel in a town miles away. She shut her door and locked it, and tried unsuccessfully to shower away the magic that still remained from the moments in Kit's arms.

CHAPTER SIX

CHARLOTTE sat beside Kit on the plane to America and sank into her own thoughts. She glanced at him now as he sat beside her in the aircraft, the inevitable papers on his lap. Wherever he was there was the briefcase, the papers and the total concentration he gave to them. She twisted the ring he had given her around on her finger, watching the light catch the stone and send out a myriad colours, its expense no longer a mystery now that she knew who he was.

Since their very brief stop at the inn by the river Kit had been cool and detached. His only aim had been to try to drill into her as much as she would need to know to carry out her duties as his wife and cause no raised eyebrows. There would be plenty though—not least of all, Brett Sanford's.

He, too, knew about her Uncle Joe. What was his attitude going to be when Kit told him that he had married Joe Roberts' niece? Her uncle was a gambler and worse! Kit came from a wealthy family with oil money behind them for many years. Why he had picked on her she did not know, except for her vulnerability and Kit's ruthless determination to have his own way. Under normal circumstances it would have been a difficult situation, but as things were Britt Sanford would pounce on her and would be watching her every move in case she showed a family weakness for other people's money.

Kit must have felt her eyes on him, his attention not

as closely on his papers as she had thought.

'Nervous, Charlotte?' He spoke without looking at her, his eyes still on his work, the endless figures, and she answered truthfully.

'A bit. I don't really know anything about where we're going and—and I don't really know what to expect. I—I mean . . .'

'I know what you mean.' He put the papers away and half turned to her. 'OK! I'll tell you everything you want to know,' he said with a patience that she found hard to believe of him. 'As to what to expect, behave as if you were my wife. Get into the habit of it. That should be enough to convince everybody. Once we're in the States, we'll fly to Baltimore and then straight down to Chesapeake.'

Chesapeake Bay. That was where Kit would take her to live, to the place he called home. She wondered if it would be home to her. There had been a few times when she had panicked at what she had done in agreeing to marry him. The main time had been when she had stood at the altar and said, 'I do.' Kit had looked down at her and she had actually felt tension in him, as if he expected her to shout 'No!' and run off. He had smiled strangely afterwards, kissing her briefly and taking her arm with a cool possessiveness, and it had been too late then to shout 'No!'

She was brewing up a burst of anxiety now, though —another one—and she marvelled at his patience with her because she was fairly sure he knew how she felt.

'Tell me about the house again,' she begged huskily, grateful that he was being for the moment so kind. 'Tell me about Markland.'

He leaned back with a laugh, his voice soft and pleasing to hear as he spoke of his house, his home that was to be her home for a while.

'It's really called Markland Creek, but mostly people just say Markland,' he told her. 'It's what is called a country estate. Really, it was a tidewater plantation, growing corn and soya, things like that, but we haven't grown anything at Markland for years. It has been in the family for generations, since colonial times, and it came to me from my father's side of the family. Now there's only my grandfather and me, but Markland is mine and mine alone, yours too now, Mrs Landor—temporarily.' He glanced across, catching her watching him with fascinated eyes, and she looked hastily away, trying not to blush but failing.

'Time was,' he continued, 'when you couldn't reach Markland in any other way but by water. Now, of course, we've progressed to roads.'

'Do you have a boat?' Charlotte asked, back to her recent occupation of watching his harshly cut, handsome face when he wasn't looking.

'Sure! We have a couple of boats—a runabout and a launch. The boathouse steps straight into the creek. You're going to enjoy your time there, Charley!'

'I hope so,' she whispered, half to herself, miserable that he was constantly reminding her of the temporary nature of their arrangement. It didn't do anything to give her confidence. 'Does your grandfather live with you?'

'Good God, no!' he said explosively. 'We get on fine from a distance, but put us both in the same house and there would be murder! And as a matter of warning, don't call him "grandfather" when you meet him. He'll get too damned cantankerous for words!'

Charlotte had a mental image of a very bad-tempered old man who growled at everyone, and she offered a prayer of thanks that he did not in fact live with Kit. It was going to be hard enough as it was, without someone else to quarrel with, someone to heartily disapprove.

'He's going to be annoyed, isn't he?' she asked quietly, and Kit shrugged as if it was no concern of his.

'He frequently is annoyed, mostly with me,' he said in an offhand voice. 'He'll get over it. Better get some rest, Charlotte,' he added suddenly, his easy tone leaving him at the mention of Brett Sanford. 'If you keep on like this you'll be worn out before we get to the East Coast.'

She tried to rest but it was impossible, and Kit was once again back with his papers. Her mind was too full of worries, too full of imagined problems.

'At this rate, we'll both be nervous wrecks,' Kit said after about twenty minutes. He put his papers away again, lowered his seat back to parallel hers and drew her into his arms, forcing her head to his shoulder. 'Go to sleep, Charlotte,' he murmured quietly. 'Nobody is going to either hurt or upset you. Just think of it all as a game, or some ordinary job.'

She closed her eyes to hide the look of hysteria. Some game! And things would be all right only as long as Kit was on her side and remembered it. She felt herself drifting off to sleep and wondered why she had suddenly relaxed. It couldn't be because he had his arm around her!

They flew from Baltimore by helicopter, a blue and silver machine that bore the name Sanford across its side. Kit introduced her to the pilot, a bronzed, good-looking young man a little older than herself who greeted Kit with a vigorous handshake and a wide grin that extended to Charlotte when she had been presented to him.

'Howdie, ma'am!'

Charlotte smiled, feeling that she had really become

Kit's wife to be addressed like that. Kit had called Mrs Atkinson 'ma'am', and she had also been greatly impressed.

'Don Segal,' Kit said, nodding to the pilot in a friendly way. 'My airborne chauffeur and general dogsbody!'

'That's me!' The young man grinned at Kit, and then turned back to the controls after giving Charlotte another admiring look as Kit settled her in the seat beside him for the flight to Markland. Her first helicopter flight ever.

It was a little frightening but tremendously exhilarating to soar over the city and then head out towards the bay, over the twin spans of the Chesapeake Bay Bridge and over the water heading seaward, down the bay to her new home. They were above water all the time, a world that was utterly new and astonishing to Charlotte, and her wide grey eyes couldn't look away.

There were islands, bright havens of emerald green among the endless blue of the water, rivers and streams that fed into the wider waters of the bay, broad streams that Kit called creeks.

'Make a sweep over Markland!' The helicopter turned at Kit's shouted command, and soon he pointed downwards as Charlotte got her first glimpse of her new home.

The land jutted out, away from the main bay, nestling into a wide creek, water on three sides. She could see that it was a grand estate, great lawns running to the water's edge, woodland scattered about the slightly rolling land. The area was flat, with miles of tidal creeks surrounding rich-looking farm land, but Markland was startlingly beautiful, like Eden in a world of water.

The house was breathtaking from this view, huge and white, like a relic from the long ago days of the Confederacy. Tall white pillars supported the roof at the front, and visions of rich ladies in extravagant gowns floated into Charlotte's dreamy mind. Shrubs and trees dotted the lawns, and across the great expanse of smoothly perfect grass, stepping out into the water as Kit had said, was a white landing-stage and boathouse. Well away from the house she could see tennis courts and, further away, a helicopter pad.

It was another world. New, wealthy and alarming.

'It's beautiful!' She only said it softly because a feeling of utter inadequacy seemed to be filling every part of her. It would have been better if she was harder, a little brash. She couldn't do this—this *job*!

Apparently Kit heard the anxiety in her voice.

'It's beautiful,' he agreed. 'It's only a house, however. You'll cope, Charlotte!'

She had thought it beautiful and it was. There was stately grandeur about the inside of the house that again seemed to come from another age; the great sweeping staircase in the magnificent hall almost looked to be part of a film set, and she knew that this house, this family, would tax all her ability to cope. This was hard to live up to, a hard act to follow even if she had really been Kit's wife.

A lady of vast proportions came bustling into the hall as Kit stood with Charlotte, giving her the chance to look around.

'Well then, Mr Kit!' she said in an accusing voice. 'I might just have known that you'd get yourself married without one word of consultation! I'm surprised you even bothered to cable you were coming!'

She was bright-faced, brightly dressed, except for her white apron, and Kit glanced apologetically at Charlotte.

'Essie!' he murmured. 'I totally forgot to tell you about Essie!'

'There!' Apparently the lady in question had sharp

ears. 'This just about shows how a body is cast aside after years of care and work. Forgot to tell her about Essie! Who runs this great barn of a place? Who's the one that's going to be expected to take care of your children like she took care of you? Forgot!'

She snorted like a steam train, and Charlotte watched her with wide and startled eyes, her expression bringing a smile to the round, red face.

'Now don't you take on, dear! Mr Kit is the one who does all these things. Ain't nothing for you to worry about! You're as pretty as a May morning!' She glared at Kit as she left. 'You done good—this time!'

Even Kit looked taken aback, and Charlotte was still waiting to hear his voice snap out at the large and bossy woman who had greeted him with this harangue. Instead he was grinning to himself, and Don Segal stuck his head into the hall.

'Is she finished?'

'For now,' Kit informed him amusedly, and Don moved back to bring in the luggage.

'I'll get this in, then, while she's still concentrating on you. I've missed out on her slamming about three times. My turn's got to be coming up soon. I'll be at the cottage if you need me.' He nodded to Charlotte and disappeared, only just in time. Essie returned with a laden trolley and shepherded them into a cosy little room off the hall.

'Time for her to go over the house when she's caught her breath!' she ordered. 'Let's get a bit of home-cooking into her first.' She hovered over Charlotte, beaming down at her as Charlotte sat unsteadily on the long, comfortable sofa. 'I made tea for you!' she boasted. 'Real English tea! It's a mercy that we got news of you in time, or lord knows what you'd have thought of us, no tea in the house and you

English!'

She turned scandalised eyes on Kit and then suddenly relented.

'You bin losing weight! Now you've got her you can settle down to being steady! All this tearing about . . .' She walked off right in the middle of her sentence and Charlotte stared at Kit.

'Is she real?' she asked in an awe-stricken voice.

'She's been real since I was ten years old, and she's not improved with the keeping,' he said drily. 'Pour the tea, for God's sake! If she comes back and finds you sitting there so pitifully, she'll swear that I've been breaking your arms!'

Charlotte poured the tea, her face losing its worried look as she began to laugh.

'She can't be that bad!'

'Better believe it!' Kit said crisply, helping himself to a large slice of apple cake. 'You've got to put your foot down in this house, Charley! Begin as you mean to go on!'

'There's not much point in that,' Charlotte said quietly. 'I won't be here long enough to make an impression.'

The smile died in Kit's eyes and he looked at her savagely.

'You're here for as long as I want you!' he bit out. 'Get this idea of a few weeks out of your head altogether! I told you that this job might take some time, and if you're going to creep around apologetically then nobody at all is going to believe that I married you. It's just not in me to marry a wet rag!'

'Having been warned of the consequences of being myself and answering back, I have little alternative but to be a wet rag!' Charlotte snapped, and to her surprise he grinned, eating his cake with relish and showing no sign of his sudden rage.

'That's better,' he said in a satisfied voice. 'Back to normal! I wouldn't want to permanently alter your character, Charley. I wouldn't want this little interlude with me to damage your spark. Apart from that, as far as anyone knows, you're the boss-lady here now. Forget that and she'll make a meal of you, me too, probably,' he added wryly.

'It's impossible to win with you, isn't it?' Charlotte snapped angrily.

'Sure is!' he drawled, standing and taking her hand. 'Start being Mrs Landor from now on. Nobody tells you what to do, except me, that is. I reserve the right to beat you from time to time. We'll work out a schedule. How would odd days suit you? Or any month with a R in it?'

She just stared at him in astonishment. Suddenly he was a very different person. It must be because he was home.

'Come on, I'll show you around a bit and then you can go to your own room and sort out your things. As matters stand, we eat at seven-thirty. You can change all that as you wish, but let it lie for now. Essie might get violent!'

Charlotte looked up at him as if she was bewitched. He was wonderful! It was impossible to keep the enchantment out of her eyes, the spellbound look from her face.

'Watch it, Charley!' he said coolly. 'There's a limit to any guarantee, and you're right here, conveniently close to hand. Remember what I told you! Don't let it slip your mind!'

She remembered. He would still divorce her, anyway. She walked around the estate with him, but her eyes really saw nothing and after a while he lost patience and dispatched her to her room and the necessary sorting of her things.

Charlotte was still sorting out her things to her own satisfaction next morning when she heard a car coming around the front of the house. It was coming fast, as if the driver was in a great hurry, almost a matter of life and death. The sound of it drew Charlotte to her window and she looked down on the front of the house.

She had a beautiful room, opposite Kit's across a wide passage that was thickly carpeted and softly lit. Her windows had a view of the creek and the boathouse, the wide stretch of water fringed with tall trees and the distant glitter of the bay itself.

They had dined alone but in great splendour, served most fussily by Essie, although Charlotte had found out by then that there were plenty of other servants and that Essie was kept busy full-time as housekeeper. Apparently, though, she wanted to be in on this herself, probably to see how she and Kit got on together. They kept up the pretence, Kit looking warningly angry whenever Charlotte seemed in danger of slipping or letting her temper override her good sense. By bedtime, Charlotte had learned a lot about the district and the history of the old house, as Kit talked easily, more easily than he had ever done before.

Presumably he was content to be home and more easy in his mind about the personal problem that Charlotte had been brought here to correct. He had said nothing, though, about a visitor, and the car that ground to a halt at the front door had also drawn Kit to the outside, although he knew quite well who to expect.

'Kit! Oh, darling, you're back! I saw the chopper come in late yesterday, but we were just going out and Eric wouldn't put it off. Oh, darling, I've missed you!'

Everything she said was breathless and worshipping,

and Charlotte's heart sank at the sight of her. This woman had a claim on Kit. It was clear from the way she looked at him, her head thrown back so that, even from here, Charlotte could see her adoring face. It was clear, too, from the way that she ran into his arms and from the way that he accepted her ecstatic greeting with a low laugh, not in any way putting her from him, that she had had plenty of encouragement.

They walked into the house together, and Charlotte knew that the next move was to call her down to meet this unexpected guest. She wanted to hide away in her lovely room, to ignore everything. How could she behave as Kit's wife when he greeted this woman with warm arms and a kiss? If she asserted herself, would he turn on her? What exactly did he expect her to do, and who was this woman in any case?

She went down, glancing at herself in the mirror before she left her room. She was a little pale and worry hadn't helped. She knew also that she had lost weight these past few days, her figure more slender than ever, the long, slim length of her legs and the beautiful curve of her neck more pronounced. The dark hair softly framed her face and her eyes were wide and clear, just faintly tinged with unease. She must not show that!

She ran lightly down the stairs and was startled to find Essie in the hall looking thunderous, her face miraculously clearing at Charlotte's determined expression. But Charlotte didn't have time to react to Essie. She smoothed her hands over the full skirt of her peach-coloured dress and walked into the room as calmly as possible, not knowing what awaited her.

Kit was just lighting a cigarette for the visitor, and her hands were clasped round his as he held his lighter for her. She was very dark, her hair almost black. Her eyes, that turned in surprise to Charlotte, were a deep brown, the darkness enhanced by skilful make-up, and she stepped back with a satisfied little smile, her hands lingering on Kit's. Whoever she was, she was staking her claim, utterly unconcerned about Charlotte's presence; she was *that* sure of herself.

Kit was looking sardonically amused, and Charlotte remembered that he had told her he would not be tied by any marriage, that if she wanted any share of his love-life she would have to join the queue. The queue was forming at once, it seemed, but she managed the best piece of acting of her whole life.

'Oh! I'm sorry, Kit! I had no idea that we had a visitor. Am I terribly late?' Amusement flared in his blue eyes, and Charlotte was glad that she was the only one to see it. It was fortunate that she was amusing him; at least she didn't have his uncertain temper to deal with as well as this visitor. But then, she reminded herself it was not too late for that temper to surface. She had known it come to the top with amazing speed.

'No, honey. Our visitor just this moment arrived. Your timing is perfect.' He walked towards her and his eyes were now watchful. This was her first big test, and she was not at all sure what the test was, as he had greeted this woman so warmly.

She was glad to feel his arm come around her as he pulled her tightly to him; temporarily then, he was on her side.

'Charley, this is Veronica Collins—she's married to an old friend of mine.' The words brought a flare of colour into the woman's face, colour that faded dramatically when he added, 'Veronica, meet Charlotte, my wife!'

There was a silence that seemed to Charlotte to be stretching into infinity, although it could only have lasted for a couple of seconds, as Veronica almost reeled from the shock. Charlotte coud see it hit her like a

physical blow, and Charlotte was equally shocked.
Veronica Collins! He had wanted a wife to get rid of this
woman, and yet he greeted her as he had done outside?
Even now, with his arm around Charlotte, he was
smiling more warmly than she had ever seen him smile!

Veronica recovered remarkably swiftly, and came
forward to shake hands, but her hand was cold and
unfriendly, her face smiling although her eyes did not.

'Well, if you say so, then I must believe it, Kit,' she
said huskily, with a quick glance at him. 'Naturally, I'm
stunned. You must forgive me, er—Charley?'

'Charlotte!' Kit said smoothly. 'I doubt if she'll
answer to Charley with anyone else but me.'

Charlotte felt like the family dog. He could have taken
advantage of that! He could have said it was his pet
name for her. It dawned on her that he was merely
playing with both of them, unless there was something
else that she had not yet seen.

'Oh! Charlotte, then.' Veronica's face regained its
composure. Subtly, Kit had made Charlotte feel too
young, inadequate, and the dread came over her that he
wasn't going to help out at all.

'She's very young, Kit,' Veronica said in an almost
dismissive voice.

'She'll get older, no doubt,' Kit assured her, smiling
down in a manner that made Charlotte uneasy. At this
rate she would be a lot older before the next hour was
up. Right now, she was standing there with his arm
around her, and however it looked to Veronica it felt
very threatening to her!

'Sit down, Veronica,' he said smoothly, adding softly,
'Let's sit over here, honey, then you can talk to your
guest nicely.' There was a softly implied threat in that,
too, and Charlotte prayed that Veronica had missed it.
Looking at her, she thought that Veronica probably had

missed it; she looked shattered and had obviously not known that Kit was married.

Essie topped off the whole bizarre preceedings by walking into the room in a manner that would have done justice to an English butler.

'Would you like me to serve tea, ma'am?' she enquired in a very elegant voice, totally at variance with her normal speech, her eyebrows raised carefully, and Charlotte swallowed her own shock and jumped quickly into the breach as Kit had an unexpected fit of coughing.

'Oh, please, Essie! That would be very nice.'

Apparently she did it rather well, because Essie smiled in a very dignified manner and left, her huge figure carried high before her like an overweight operatic singer. Charlotte felt bemused, and Kit draped his arm across her shoulders, his fingers lightly stroking her neck.

'Well, then, Veronica, how's my good friend Eric?' he said sardonically, and Charlotte knew that she was only a bystander in this, a mere pawn in the game. In spite of her attempt to keep upright, her shoulders drooped.

Afterwards it was difficult to remember what they had talked about. Instinctively she knew that only Kit was enjoying this, that Veronica would have given anything to have never been here at all. She was waiting to speak to Kit alone, and every word she uttered seemed to be ammunition for Kit's guns.

'I wonder how you've survived the meeting with Kit's grandfather,' she said with a long, considering look at Charlotte as she sat securely against Kit. 'I imagine you *have* told him?' she added, glancing at Kit with the sparkle of malice in her dark eyes.

'I cabled him from London as soon as we were married,' Kit said evenly. 'He'll be here very soon, I've no doubt about that. He's always been very particular about who I eventually married!'

'Yes!' The flat statement told Charlotte so much. Brett Sanford did not like Veronica, then. He would not have approved of any match between Kit and this woman.

'I wonder what he'll think of Charlotte?' Veronica asked sweetly, her face amused already at the explosion she seemed to know would come from Brett Sanford.

'He'll take to her!' Kit said mockingly. 'Her uncle is an old buddy of his. But even if he doesn't, it's a little too late. I already married her!'

Charlotte's blood ran cold. Was Kit about to tell this woman about her uncle? Even if he did not, how long would it be before everyone knew? Brett Sanford knew, and he was no longer a frind of her uncle; he was going to put him in jail if Kit told him where Joe Roberts was!

'He never took to me!' Veronica said bitterly, and Charlotte spoke up, angry at being the pig-in-the-middle in this game they were playing.

'But I'm *married* to Kit,' she said sharply. 'He will naturally make an effort with Kit's wife!'

Veronica laughed sharply, a sound like broken glass.

'I can see you haven't told Charlotte in any depth about Brett's worst characteristics,' she murmured sarcastically, getting to her feet. 'I wish I could be there! I'd love to see the old devil's face.'

'I expect to win him over!' Charlotte said firmly. 'In any case, he might surprise everyone and become my champion!'

'It will certainly surprise everyone!' Veronica said sharply.

'It won't surprise me,' Kit said in a mocking voice. 'She's young and beautiful. He always had an eye for youth and beauty. I even fancy her myself!' he finished, dropping a quick, hard kiss on Charlotte's lips before going to the door with Veronica.

The fury on the older woman's face was barely contained, and Kit flashed a look at Charlotte.

'I'll see Veronica out,' he said with that tone in his voice that made it an order. 'You curl up here, I'll be back.'

Curl up was exactly what she wanted to do, because she hadn't missed the tension in the air and she could hear their voices outside, a fact that didn't seem to have dawned on either of them.

'Tell Eric that I expect to see him very soon,' he said. 'We'll all get together for dinner one night.'

'Yes, I'll tell him,' Veronica answered in a low voice, adding in a voice that was even lower, but quite audible to Charlotte, 'What are you up to, Kit? How could you do this? You never play anything straight down the middle, do you?'

Kit laughed in that quiet and alarming way of his.

'No unless I have to, and certainly not when it's impossible! You surely knew that I'd marry one day?'

'Kit, you and I . . . I know that Brett hates me, but . . .'

'I take his point! You're married to Eric! Remember him?' Kit bit out. 'How long did you think I was going to let this go on?'

Veronica's car left with a squeal of tyres that emphasised her distress, and Charlotte suddenly knew exactly why Kit had wanted a wife.

He came back into the room, his eyes piercingly blue on her, seeing exactly what was on her face and liking it not at all.

'Is that it, then?' Charlotte asked, trembling angry. 'Can I now stand down from my post? After all, she did sound the retreat very loudly!'

'Did she bother you?' He walked across and cupped her hot, angry face in his hands, looking down intently into her eyes, his voice filled with derision. 'Yes, you can stand down, Charlotte. The enemy is in full retreat and you hardly fired a shot.'

'You did that well enough by springing me on her like that!' Charlotte snapped, her face clouded with anger and an inner hurt that he could feel nothing for her when she was beginning to . . .

She tore herself away and he let her go, but he was angry, she could see that.

'What did you expect me to do?' he asked savagely, his voice low. 'Should I have sent her a cable? Should I have told her to brace herself? I've been bracing myself ever since she married Eric!'

'Why didn't you marry her yourself?' Charlotte said angrily, her misery just about overflowing.

'Too big a price to pay!' he sneered, his face cold. 'Besides, my best friend wanted her and Brett can't stand the sight of her!'

'So now you just have . . .' Charlotte began sarcastically, but he pounced on her like a tiger.

'Not another word, Charlotte!' he warned with a sinister quiet, his hands tightly on her arms. 'I'm through threatening you! Next words out of place and you get action!' He suddenly relaxed, seeing the misery on her face, no doubt, and he gave a twisted smile. 'Youth and beauty beat sophistication hands down, flowerface,' he said mockingly. 'You've got all the big guns on your side. Brett is really going to go for you in a big way!'

'And leave you free to follow whatever devious path you choose!' Charlotte snapped. 'I wonder which way the guns will turn when you divorce me?'

She twisted away and walked off. It was all too clear at last. Kit had not married Veronica because his grandfather hated her. Veronica's greeting and his acceptance of it showed that there was still something between them. Well, she wouldn't help! Kit could carry on exactly as he liked and she would play the dumb little wife! She didn't know Eric Collins. He could take care of himself! All she was bothered about was keeping her uncle out of jail. As to Kit's grandfather, he could like her or not as he chose, but she wasn't about to cover for Kit and the woman.

It was painfully clear why Kit had wanted a wife so quickly, someone young and gullible enough to be fooled into coming here, someone vulnerable who owed him a great deal. He could do as he liked now, without Eric suspecting a thing! A dreadful pain stabbed inside her, twisting and burning, and she recognised it, although she had never felt it before in her life. Jealousy! *She* was Kit's wife, and she wanted to be his wife so hungrily that the realisation made her feel faint.

CHAPTER SEVEN

LATE in the afternoon, Charlotte heard a helicopter coming in and went to the window. She saw it skim in over the creek and move like a busy wasp towards the pad and, almost at once, Kit knocked on her door and strode in.

'Brett's here!' he said coldly, his eyes on her jeans and bright-coloured top.

'I never heard Don take the helicopter to fetch him from the airport,' Charlotte remarked, looking up from the book she had purposefully picked up as she heard Kit striding towards her room.

'We've got more than one helicopter!' he rasped, looking as if he doubted her sanity. 'He's here, anyway! Get ready!'

'The sackcloth or the tiara?' Charlotte asked sweetly, and the blue eyes narrowed dangerously.

For one wild moment she thought he was going to walk further in and slap her, but his mouth suddenly quirked and his gaze ran over her slender, defiant figure.

'OK, Miss Prim,' he murmured mockingly. 'You think you can handle Brett Sanford? Get to it! This I've got to see!'

He went without waiting for her at all and she felt decidedly less bold without him. She went to the mirror and looked seriously at her reflection. She was herself, a girl from a small town, from an ordinary job, who had lived an ordinary life until Kit had moved into it. If Brett Sanford disliked her, then it was just too bad! She went downstairs with nothing but grim determination on her face, not even one bit scared when she found him already in there, sitting on the long settee in the drawing-room, his eyes narrowed and cold as Kit's.

He stood slowly as she came into the room, and Charlotte got quite a shock. The grumpy old man she had expected to see was not there, and her mind had to make a rapid re-assessment. He was tall as Kit, his hair thick and white. He had the same brilliantly blue eyes and he was really handsome. Power radiated from him and wealth, and Charlotte knew that this man would be a deadly enemy or a great friend; there was no compromise in him.

Kit moved towards her at once, his arm coming round her. At any other time she would have been glad of it, but today she had faced just about all she intended to face, and her expression was as cold as Brett Sanford's.

'So this is your wife?' His voice was as powerful as his appearance, and his eyes held hers relentlessly.

'This is Charlotte!' Kit agreed with a real bite to his voice, his hand tightening on her as he stood watching his grandfather's face with a look of aggression.

'You think you're good enough for my grandson?' Brett Sanford asked coolly and Charlotte's voice was equally cool.

'Much better, Mr Sanford!' she assured him flatly. 'I don't tell lies! Kit pretended to be an accountant until after we were married—even then, somebody else had to tell me what I'd let myself in for. You'll understand, of course, that it has left me wary! I'm not at all sure that you are who you say you are!'

There was a moment of stunned silence, and then the eyes that watched her narrowed to points of blue light.

'So you didn't marry him for his money, then?' he asked with just the fine edge of insult.

'No,' Charlotte assured him with a faint smile. 'I had an entirely different motive!'

He just looked at her steadily, and Charlotte became aware that Kit's hand had tightened on her to the point of real pain. He wondered what she was going to say next. Let him wonder! She suddenly saw a weapon of her own. How would Brett Sanford like it if his new granddaughter had an uncle in prison? Deceived or not, she was Kit's wife for now and, like it or not, his grandfather had to accept that fact. She wondered how he would take to the idea that this was a game, a ploy to go on seeing a married woman. It brought a wry smile to her face, in spite of her inner nervousness. With a few words she could floor them both! 'By the way, Mr Sanford, Kit hired me to be his wife. He's mixed up with a married lady!' She could just imagine the reaction from both of them.

'And what are you laughing at, young lady?' Brett Sanford suddenly barked. 'Do you realise that Kit has been and got himself married without any thought as to how I'd take it? I wasn't even invited to the wedding of my only grandson!'

'I'm sorry that you weren't at the wedding, but then, I had no relative there either. We could get married again if you want,' Charlotte said pleasantly, her smile growing at the utter astonishment of these two aggressive men.

He looked at her as if she was a totally unexpected phenomenon, insolently mad, dangerously careless of her personal safety, and his eyes moved to Kit with a sort of ferocious astonishment.

'I hope to God she's on your side, boy!' he grated. 'You've married yourself a fire-cracker!'

It suddenly dawned on Charlotte that Kit was laughing quietly, some of the tension leaving him.

Knowing her as he seemed to, he had probably realised what had been running through her mind, and the fact that she had stopped short of saying it must be a relief of some magnitude.

'So! You think insolence is funny!' Brett Sanford snapped, his sharp eyes on Kit's face. 'I hope you think she's worth all the trouble she's going to cause!'

'She's above price,' Kit said softly. 'She's going to grow on you!'

'Come here, girl, and let's have a look at you!' Brett Sanford suddenly snapped, and Kit moved with her, his hand still possessively on her, but all he got was a bark of annoyance.

'Let her walk by herself, for God's sake! She doesn't look as if she's got anything wrong with her legs! There's certainly nothing wrong with her tongue!'

Charlotte went forward alone as Kit very reluctantly let her go. She was not afraid of Brett Sanford, or anyone else for that matter! She wasn't going to step from one sort of fear in England to have another sort of fear here. She held a few cards of her own. Her clear grey eyes held the keen blue gaze of Kit's grandfather, and she walked towards him until she was looking up into his face.

'She's a pretty little thing,' he conceded, talking as if she wasn't there, 'potential of real beauty.'

'She's got that already!' Kit cut in crisply.

'She's certainly got an impudent tongue,' Brett admitted, looking at her as if she was in a sale. 'Come here, girl!' he ordered, gathering her into two amazingly strong arms. He kissed her cheek and then held her at arm's length, looking at her sternly. 'I suppose we'll have to make the best of you as we've got you! Don't call me grandfather!' he ordered.

'I haven't!' she answered pertly. 'I shall call you

Mr Sanford!'

'Brett! If you know what's good for you!' he growled.

'Not until we're friends,' Charlotte said firmly. 'I can't pretend feelings that I don't have.'

He looked as if he was going to explode, but a slow smile of reluctant admiration spread across his fine face.

'Well, you don't scare, do you?' he muttered quietly. 'I might make something of you, at that!'

Not when he found out that she was merely a hostage for her uncle, Charlotte thought grimly, but Essie chose that moment to come in and beam at Brett.

'I got all your favourites, Mr Sanford!' she promised, but before his grandfather could reply Kit laid down strict orders.

'We're eating at the club tonight, Essie,' he said in a voice that even she dared not quetion. 'I want Charley to meet everyone,' he added for Brett's benefit, as Essie made a grumpy retreat. Brett nodded in understanding, his eyes on Charlotte still.

'That's what you call her—Charley?' he asked with deep interest.

'When she's very good,' Kit agreed sardonically, with a slanting look at Charlotte's mutinous face.

'That's what I'll call her!' Brett said firmly. 'I kind of like it. Charley! It's easy on the tongue. Mind you, if she wasn't such a beauty . . .'

'Yeah!' Kit agreed in his normally laconic way.

And then they both seemed to dismiss her with unspoken accord.

'Come into the study,' Kit said quietly. 'I've got a few things to talk over with you.'

Brett nodded politely but curtly to Charlotte, and Kit gave her a look that might well have been threatening; she didn't care. She was quite finished with any sort of submission. She went to her room, unhappy about Kit but quite pleased with her own stand against Brett Sorford. One bully was enough for anyone!

It was some time later that Kit came up, and he walked in after the most brief tap on her door.

'You seem to enjoy living on the edge of danger,' he bit out at once. 'Am I to take it that there was a threat intended down there?'

'You can take it however you like!' Charlotte answered angrily. 'Your grandfather is a very rude man! If you think that I'm going to put up with his bullying as well as yours, then think again!'

'Bullying?' Kit said in amused surprise. 'He was just a little stunned, but he took to you at once when you stood up to him.'

'I couldn't care less!' Charlotte snapped. 'I'm here and I have to stay, but I really don't care what anyone thinks or does!'

'Really?' Kit was suddenly towering over her, and some of the defiance left her face. 'Then you'll not care what I do, will you?'

'No, I won't!' Charlotte flared.

'In that case, don't mind this!' Kit grated, pulling her into his arms and capturing her lips at once.

She was too angry to be bewitched, though, this time, and she fought wildly. He simply held her, his lips hard on hers until she had fought herself to a standstill, her breath no more than shallow murmurs against his mouth.

'Now, Charley,' he said softly, 'let's see what you don't care about!'

It was too late to beg for mercy. Defiance brought its own rules, and she had laid down those rules herself, Kit was not about to listen to any pleas. His head lowered slowly to hers, and as his lips began to explore her flushed face the hard arms relaxed to gentleness.

'I'm not hurting you, Charley,' he murmured against her lips, and she had to admit to herself that he was r t. He was soothing, drugging, and she totally forgot to hate him, her wild fight far away, drifting from the back of her mind into oblivion.

When his lips closed over hers, her mouth opened sweetly and his tongue teased the inner warmth of it until her breath was merely a moan of pleasure. She had no idea that they were so close to her bed until he moved back, taking her with him, his lips still teasing hers as she murmured worriedly.

'It's all right, Charley,' he said against her lips. 'Don't fight me.'

She remembered then that she should be fighting, but his searching hand had moved beneath her soft, bright shirt to cup and mould her breast, and she forgot again as his fingers stroked its peak to hard arousal. Everything was pleasure, a spiralling delight that grew into frenzy as his lips followed his fingers to taste gently and then deeply as he pushed her shirt high and grasped her small waist with determined hands, his mouth on her breast with an almost desperate urgency . . .

'Kit! No!' Her wild cry had his head lifting, his eyes feverishly on hers before his lips, hot and demanding, silenced her cry. For a moment she melted, everything forgotten now, and her acquiescence was accepted at once as Kit's hand slid over her flat stomach to tug impatiently at her belt.

It was his impatience that awakened her instincts of self-preservation. Her mind noticed that he was no longer gentle, and that word alone alerted her.

'Of course I'm gentle! I'm seducing you!'

Memory raced across her mind, and she rolled away from him so swiftly that he was taken by surprise. She was on her feet, looking at him in horror, before he had recovered from the shock of her going.

He said nothing. He simply sat up, his eyes intent on her pale face, and then he slowly stood to tower over her.

'Next time, Charley,' he breathed thickly, 'I'll take you. Nobody teases me!'

He strode from the room and she had to shake off the guilty feeling. She had not teased him! He had once again tried to break the bargain—simply because she was there. Bitterness washed over her and she paced about the room telling herself that she hated Kit Landor, but she knew it was not true. It was impossible to lie to herself.

She got ready for dinner in a bemused state, admitting that the vague fright that she still felt was really a delicious feeling. Since their rather angry encounter Kit had behaved perfectly normally, talking to her as if nothing at all had happened when she went downstairs for afternoon tea, and she had been too wary to continue any argument, too wary to continue, either, with any immediate battle with Brett.

She had found Brett Sanford watching her with a new look in his eyes. It amounted to amused speculation, and she imagined that she must be an unusual oddity.

She took the turquoise dress from her wardrobe now and held it in front of her. It had been cleaned to perfection in the London hotel, every mark gone. It looked new. To her, though, it still spelled catastrophe—but it was so beautiful. The other dresses she had bought were equally beautiful, but the turquoise dress was a challenge. When she had worn it before she had simply given in and run. It was like a red rag to a bull. She would never again be able to even see the colour without remembering the incident. She set her lips determinedly and left it out ready.

'Charlotte, it's time!' Kit called to her after tapping on her door, no desire in him apparently to now just stride inside, and she took a last glance at herself before moving to open the door for him.

'Tempting fate, Charley?' he asked with a wry grin, his eyes skimming over her as she stood young and beautiful in the doorway, her eyes just a little determined and glittery. 'I had the feeling that you'd wear that. Come back inside.'

She stepped back into her room, suddenly trembling and he followed, reaching into his pocket to take out a leather box, opening it and putting it on the dressing-table.

'I got you these for tonight,' he said quietly.

The box held a necklace and matching ear-rings, diamonds that caught the light and glittered with a dazzling fire.

'Oh! I can't! I can't possibly . . .'

'You're supposed to be my wife, Charlotte!' he said with a sudden anger. 'You *are* my wife, even if it's all a charade. I'm rich! People will expect to see you drenched in diamonds, and you're going to be!'

He turned her none too gently and fastened the necklace himself as she stood trembling, holding each ear-ring until she had them fixed, and then turning her to the mirror to look. They were perfect, coldly beautiful against the colour of her dress; the design of the jewellery was young and eye-catching.

'There,' he said in a satisfied voice. 'When this is over, you can keep them, along with anything else I give you—an extra reward.'

'I—I don't need rewards. I never will,' she said in a low voice, trembling now that his hands were no longer against her skin, admitting that these feelings were geting out of her control.

His palms came to rest lightly on her bare shoulders, and his thumbs were unconsciously stroking against her neck.

'I know. That's why you're likely to get plenty of them,' he said, his eyes meeting hers through the mirror. 'Let me have a look at the whole effect. We want to dazzle Brett, after all.'

He let her go and she spun slowly round to face him as he stood a little way back, looking at her.

'Young as the spring,' he said quietly. 'You're going to have no trouble at all fooling people, Charley.'

Only myself, she thought, her face clouding, looking away hastily as a very wary look came into his eyes.

The club was not the sort of stuffy place that she had vaguely imagined from her limited knowledge of the grand life. She had hazily thought of a kind of quiet and plush place solely for men, the sort of atmosphere where Sherlock Holmes would not have felt out of place. She was wrong. It was a place where rich men took their guests, met their friends and rivals, and she was glad of both the lovely dress and the diamonds. Kit had known exactly what she would face, and she offered a prayer that there would be no accidental spilling of soup tonight.

Kit was greeted like royalty, especially by some of the very glamorous women there. She had never before seen so many beautiful women all seemingly intent on gaining the attention of one man. He sailed through it with a wry smile and a few amused words, but it left her feeling very vulnerable. He could have the choice of at least ten women here, from the look in their eyes. He had told her that much himself, and apparently it was no idle boast.

Brett was greeted with surprise and a good deal of awe; apparently he did not come here often now, and he was soon surrounded by people who wanted his opinion on business that was not even oil.

He surprised her, though. He spent ages showing her off to his friends, until she became quite blasé about the whole thing, Brett on one side and Kit on the other. A couple of drinks helped of course, and by the time that they sat down to dinner she was quite warm inside, both with the drinks and with the constant praise that Brett poured over her, even if it was only for the benefit of strangers and to show that the family stood as one. She had no doubt about Kit. He was making certain that everyone knew he had a wife.

Even if her thoughts had been mere suspicions, they were confirmed later as Veronica Collins stopped as she passed their table.

'Well, Kit!' she gasped in greatly exaggerated surprise. 'I had no idea you would be here tonight!'

'Just showing Charley off to everyone,' Kit said smoothly, coming to his feet. Brett stood too, but with very obvious reluctance. 'Eric here?' Kit asked.

'No, I'm with friends! How are you, Brett?' There was just the glitter of unease in her eyes as she turned to Kit's grandfather, and he did nothing to disappoint her.

'Enjoying having dinner with my granddaughter!' he stated coolly. 'You tell Eric I want to see him—if your paths finally cross!'

'I'll do that!' she snapped, moving off, but Charlotte saw Kit's eyes follow her, and her heart sank even more. This was where they met, then, casually and openly, bumping into each other with great surprise. Veronica had not expected Kit's wife to be here, neither had she expected to see Brett.

Someone called to Kit and he left the table for a

minute to cross the room, but he stopped by Veronica's friends on the way back and she could see him smiling. Brett met her eyes and then looked away angrily.

'Do you love my hard-bitten grandson?' he suddenly muttered, his eyes flashing up to her from beneath thick brows.

'I married him!' Charlotte said evenly, meeting his keen eyes.

He nodded slowly, a faint smile edging his mouth.

'You're a fighter, girl!' he assured her. 'I guess you'll do, after all!'

His hand covered her slim fingers and as she looked at him with startled eyes she suddenly knew that Brett was well aware of the feelings between Kit and Veronica Collins, and he liked it not at all. She had found a friend. After that he was charm itself, warm as she had never imagined possible from her first meeting with him. As they rose to leave and he went to say goodbye to an old friend, Kit helped Charlotte to her feet, moving the chair and standing dutifully behind her as she stood.

'Well, well!' he jeered. 'The old bear has taken to the child bride, then?'

'I'm not a child!' she mutteed heatedly, and his laughter was utterly derisive.

'Is that a fact?' he murmured, and she almost jumped out of her skin when he dropped a kiss on her smooth shoulder.

She blushed wildly, but she knew exactly what it was. The whole of the club was looking on as far as she could tell. No doubt the word would spread rapidly. Kit Landor married and deeply in love! No doubt Brett would spread the news himself. He looked like a dog with two tails. He was beaming at them across the room, and Veronica Collins was watching with eyes as derisive as Charlotte knew Kit's would be if she turned to face him!

CHAPTER EIGHT

SHE had never expected that the Collinses would come to dinner, not so soon. In her place, Charlotte knew that she would never have set foot in Markland again, but then, she wasn't in love with someone else's wife as Kit was, and it was clear that Veronica had seen the reason for Kit's marriage in the meantime; maybe he had even telephoned her and explained, or explained at the club. Whatever had happened, two days later the invitation was accepted, and Kit's friend Eric came to Markland with his wife beside him.

Brett had gone, but during his brief stay he had accepted Charlotte in a way that she found unbelievable.

'Soon, Charley,' he had said as he left, 'I'll get Kit to bring you to Huston, and you'll stay with me in the penthouse. I'll really get to know my new grand-daughter!'

He had hugged her warmly, kissing her cheek, and she suddenly found herself tearful at the idea of his going. Instinctively she knew that he was someone she could appeal to, someone to rely on as she had once relied on Kit. She watched rather wistfully as the helicopter climbed from Markland and headed out over the creek, and Kit's arm came round her, although she knew it was merely in case Brett should still be watching.

'That didn't take long, did it?' he murmured sardonically, his normal attitude since she had repulsed him so firmly. 'To convert Brett in such a short time is a great

133

feat. Obviously you're a man after his own heart!' he sneered.

'Nothing magical!' Charley snapped. 'He fondly imagines that I love you!'

It was a stupid thing to say. Idiotic! She had thought that by now she had her unruly tongue under control, but apparently she had not.

'He must be getting old at last!' Kit snarled, letting her go and striding off without her. 'Time was when nobody could pull the wool over Brett Sanford's eyes. Luckily you won't have to keep it up too long!'

She watched his tall, hard figure striding away, thankful that he had gone ahead. If he ever discovered that she *did* love him, he would take advantage of it at once!

Although Essie had said nothing outright, her attitude when Veronica had arrived unexpectedly had shown Charlotte that she greatly disapproved. This disapproval did not, however, extend itself to Eric Collins, because when Charlotte, in her new role of mistress of Markland, informed Essie that there would be two more for dinner and told her who they were, she smiled in a reminiscent way.

'Mr Eric! That boy! He was as close as a brother to Mr Kit. They were happy as the day until . . .' She closed her mouth firmly and Charlotte knew that she was going to get nothing else. She wanted nothing else, anyway. She knew in her heart that Eric Collins had married the woman that Kit wanted for himself. Kit was not the sort to sit and weep over this sort of thing; he had made his own plans.

'How did Brett take to you?' Eric asked, smiling down at Charlotte after they had been introduced. He was tall and well built, Kit's age by the look of him, and the overall impression that Charlotte got was 'pleasant'. With dark curly hair, rather large spectacles and a sunny smile, he was impossible to dislike.

His greeting of Kit had been one of great friendliness, so there was obviously no animosity there. The secret between Kit and Veronica was with them alone. Eric knew nothing, that much was clear.

'Brett is bowled over!' Kit said with a laugh as he poured drinks. He was very pleasant to Veronica tonight, and Charlotte knew that her own presence here would have made almost anything possible without Eric being suspicious. It made things seem worse than ever to her, though.

'Brett never liked me, of course,' Veronica put in with a little laugh. 'I never could please him.'

'Not many people can, darling,' Eric said with a smile at her. 'Don't take it to heart. Brett Sanford makes his own rules.'

'He liked you well enough!' Veronica said a trifle sharply, but this time it was Kit who answered.

'Eric was more or less one of the family from being about ten years old. Brett doesn't take too well to women unless he chooses them himself.'

'Well, he didn't choose you, Charlotte!' Veronica pointed out with a rather wild little laugh. 'You must tell me your secret!'

'Charley went for him with all guns blazing!' Kit said with a quizzical smile. 'He fell for her straight away.'

'You went for Brett Sanford? This I must hear about!' Eric took her arm and looked very interested, but Kit interrupted at once.

'You'll get no family gossip out of Charley, Eric. She's loyal and discreet, and now that she's related to Brett there'll be no way that she'll gossip at all. One thing about Charley, you can turn your back on her without any qualms. I'd trust her with my life!'

'What an odd thing to say, darling!' Veronica said

with a brittle laugh as Eric looked astonished. 'She sounds more like a secretary than a wife! How did she capture you?'

Charlotte's heart seemed to be somewhere in her throat, but Kit looked across at her with a quirk to his hard lips.

'She blazed away at me, too,' he said softly. 'Obviously it's a family weakness!'

Essie came to announce dinner and Charlotte was never so glad. Essie hovered around too, quite unforgivably but Charlotte forgave her gladly. Her presence made any further conversation of an intimate variety out of the question. As for Kit, he never seemed to notice that Essie was there at all. Charlotte was stunned that Eric appeared to be in complete ignorance of the deep, underlying feelings that were filtering through the room.

Of course, this made it necessary for Charlotte to speak to Veronica for most of the time. She was a very complex kind of woman, Charlotte decided. With Kit fully occupied, she appeared to feel it necessary to pry.

'You'll be finding Essie a handful, I expect,' she murmured derisively as Essie left them for a while, being unable to find any excuse for lingering further. It did not fool Charlotte. Veronica was pointing out how unsuitable she was to be Kit's wife, how young, how very much out of his bracket.

'I was a little overwhelmed at first,' Charlotte confessed, making her mind up that she was going to do not one single thing to help Kit out. 'Now, though, she takes a delight in mothering me, and I don't mind that too much for now.'

'Perhaps you'll get your foot in sooner or later,' Veronica said with a sweet smile. 'You're new and a little young, but she'll have to accept you as Kit's wife eventually. She needed someone with a great deal of experience to keep her in her place, of course.'

Like you? Charlotte thought, but she stayed silent. She was all too aware that she was not experienced, and that she didn't particularly fit in here in this splendid house. Right now, she felt like a stray puppy that Kit had found and brought home. She did not want to put Essie in her place. As far as Charlotte was concerned, Essie *was* in her place. She had mothered Kit for most of his life, and clearly she cared about him. As for herself, she had had rather enough of mothering her Uncle Joe, so Essie's attention was not at all displeasing. In any case, how long would she be here?

'By the way,' Kit said a little later when they were ready to go, 'we're having a party to introduce Charlotte to the folks around here. I figured that next weekend would be a good time. You'll come, of course!'

He wasn't asking at all, Charlotte marvelled. It was an order. He was just like his grandfather!'

'Wouldn't miss it for the world!' Eric said gleefully before Veronica could even speak. What answer Veronica would have given, Charlotte did not know, but she saw her eyes meet Kit's for a second and then saw her face colour swiftly. Kit wanted to let everyone see his wife. Only Eric missed all the intrigue. Charlotte's heart sank. His plans were going to be put into action at once. If anyone saw him with Veronica later they would dismiss it; after all, he had a wife who was young, beautiful and English. Nobody would give credence to any affair.

'I wonder if Brett will come?' Charlotte said rather wistfully, wanting an ally suddenly, and Kit put his arm around her and kissed her cheek.

'You know that he will if you drop the hint, sweetheart,' he said in such a loving manner that she cringed inside. She went to bed more miserable than she had ever been in her life.

Kit sauntered into her room as she was cleansing her face for bed. He leaned against the dressing-table, looking down at her as she sat in her robe, her hands busily wiping off make-up.

'Well, what do you think of Eric?' he asked casually. 'I noticed that you charmed him. You spent a lot of time talking to him, too.'

'Somebody had to take care of the poor man!' Charlotte snapped, ignoring Kit's narrowed eyes as he noted her attitude. 'As you were busy charming Veronica in dulcet tones, I decided to play hostess!'

'And judge and executioner!' he sneered. 'I gave you credit for some brains, Charlotte!'

'Did you?' she asked sweetly, turning to him with a sarcastic look. 'Obviously you were wrong, otherwise I wouldn't be here. When you've a minute, get a calendar and work out the time I've still got to serve, will you?'

'I can tell you right off the top of my head!' he rasped, jerking her to her feet and into his arms. 'For ever, if it suits me!'

'I can't be intimidated!' Charlotte gasped frantically, struggling furiously to free herself. 'As soon as my uncle is in no danger . . .'

'I'll see that he stays exactly as he is!' Kit murmured mockingly. 'I'll do anything I have to do to get my own way, Charlotte!' he jeered softly.

'Supposing that I tell Brett?' Charlotte threatened, and he let her go with a cold laugh.

'And have him demand to be told where I've stashed Joe?' he enquired scathingly. 'Well, you can always try it! You've seen Brett, though. How long do you think it would be before Joe was in court? Brett is tough as they come, and not much heart in him when it comes to the oil business. He's fought to keep everything he inherited, to pass it on to me. No crook is going to get it away from him, and no crook is going to get away without punishment! Still, you can try it! He likes you, he even admires you!'

'Does—does he know who I am?' Charlotte asked a little fearfully.

'Do I look stupid?' he ground out. 'He never asked your second name, and I never informed him. Putting two and two together has never been much trouble to Brett!'

He just stormed off out of the room, and Charlotte was left more uneasy than ever. The ball seemed to be back with Kit. If she asked for help from Brett Sanford, then her uncle would be in jail before she could even get back home. She would have to live through this all by herself.

Next morning Charlotte was up early. The heat of the sun through her window had made her wake up, and she stood for a minute looking across to the water that glittered so invitingly. The little landing-stage was dappled in the shadows of trees, and she had the urge to walk there and stand beside the side, swiftly moving creek. She put on her shorts and a thin cotton shirt, and as soon as she had eaten breakfast she was out across the lawns, walking along the short pier to the boathouse.

Kit had been up an hour earlier and had already gone off somewhere, Essie had told her, but she didn't want to think about Kit. In any case, she had not dared to enquire further. As Kit's wife, it was to be expected that she would know where he was, and Essie already disapproved of the fact that there were two bedrooms instead of one matrimonial room. Of course, she had said nothing, but it was there in her face.

Last night's events had cast a great shadow on

Charlotte. Deep down she had admitted to being in love with Kit long ago, but now it was there out in the open, too powerful to ignore, too hurtful to think about. She blamed Kit for everything. If he had not behaved as he had, forcing her to be with him, forcing her into this marriage, she would have already forgotten him. Her head insisted that it was true, although her mind knew that it wasn't.

There was no forgiveness in her for the way he treated her, either. Maybe he did want her, but only because she was right there under his nose. She refused to be a substitute for Veronica Collins! Somehow she had to get out of this without damaging her uncle in any way. It would take some thinking about and, as yet, nothing suggested itself to her except that at the back of her mind she felt that Brett would help if she really explained. He would be furious, though, at the deception. He was not a man to take lightly to anything like this, and there was a very real chance that in spite of her name being involved, and with it Kit's, his anger would direct itself immediately at her uncle.

There was a bright red speed-boat tied to the landing-stage, and she supposed that this was what Kit had referred to as the runabout. She climbed across carefully to the boathouse, hoping to see the launch, but there was nothing there, only the usual tackle that went with boats and boating.

She was just standing looking down at the water, her arms along the rail of the landing-stage, when she heard footsteps behind her and looked around to see Don Segal approaching.

'Oh! Good morning!' She managed a brilliant smile and he came to stand beside her, his eyes a little intent.

'Morning, Mrs Landor! You're up bright and early.'

'I had the urge to see the boats, but there's only one

here,' she said with a laugh. 'And please call me Charlotte.'

'OK, Charlotte,' he grinned. 'Don't know if the boss will approve, but I'll take the chance.'

Charlotte forbore to tell him what the boss could do, and turned her gaze on to the red boat. In point of fact, Don was making her feel a little embarrassed, and she was wishing herself back in the house with Essie.

'You look about thirteen,' he said with a laugh that contained more excitement than was proper in her opinion, and she could actually feel his gaze roaming over her slender legs in the white shorts, and the way her hair was tied back into a ponytail.

'Well, I don't feel it,' she said as lightly as she could, furious with herself for getting into this situation. Were all men as bad as this? First Kit and now Don Segal. 'It—it must be lovely to be able to simply skim out over the water,' she ventured shakily, searching frantically for a topic of safe conversation.

'Take the boat out!' he said promptly. 'It's pretty safe so long as you don't go too far.'

'It's not as easy as that!' Charlotte almost snapped, feeling more trapped than ever when she realised that she had no idea how to even start the boat—she couldn't even drive a car! 'I suppose you've grown up with boats. I lived in a small town in England, well inland.'

'I'll take you, no big deal!' he said eagerly. 'The boss isn't here this morning. He might be back later, but there's time.'

No, he wasn't here! Where would he be? She didn't have to think too deeply. Eric would be at work, whatever he did—a lawyer, hadn't Kit said? Lawyers went to their office, wives stayed at home. It didn't take too much imagination to guess where Kit was! Unfortunately, once started, her imagination refused to stop, and she could see Veronica in Kit's arms just as *she* had been in his arms.

'You're on!' she said with a great deal of gaiety.

'Right!' Don was grinning all over his face, and handed Charlotte into the gleaming, red boat, turning to untie it at once.

'Have you run out of work?'

The hard voice was like a whiplash and Don looked up, red-faced, clearly not used to being addressed in such tones. Charlotte too felt a little like coming to attention at the sound of Kit's angry voice, but she held her ground and met his furious eyes with a cool gaze that apparently infuriated him further.

'Couldn't find you,' Don said with a return to good humour. 'Charlotte wanted a quick spin in the runabout.'

'Don't let *my wife* occupy your valuable time!' Kit bit out, his eyes narrowing at Don's familiarity. 'I'm sure there's plenty for you to do if you look around!'

'OK.' To Charlotte's surprise, Don's shrug was all good humour. 'What's a dogsbody for, after all?' He handed Charlotte back out of the boat, gave her a small ironic bow and sauntered off.

Charlotte attempted the same thing, but got no further than two steps.

'Don't encourage Don!' Kit snarled, grabbing her arm and swinging her to face him.

'He was being kind to me!' Charlotte snapped, angrily trying to detach herself from his grip, a thing that she realised furiously was a frequent task.

'I can imagine!' he rasped, his eyes running insultingly over her slender figure, lingering on her legs. 'What do you expect when you come out like that? You look about sixteen!'

'Oh? Don put it at thirteen!' Charlotte remarked

calmly, and almost ducked as his eyes threatened to kill her.

He looked so handsome and so particularly devilish this morning that she dared not look too closely at him. Her heart was taking on that peculiar hammering again, and her face flushed when she saw his eyes on the heavy rise and fall of her breasts.

'So you want a spin in the boat?' he asked softly. 'That's easily done. This way, my lady!'

He had leapt into the boat, lifted her in, untied and started the engine before she could get her breath, and she sat down rapidly, hanging on to the rail as she realised the rage that was in him. This was not going to be a nice morning spin on the water. He looked as if he might ram something, and she could see his point. It wouldn't look too good if she was seen with another man. Charlotte in the foreground, Veronica in the background! Her temper rose to the top.

The boat more or less leapt free, turning and heading down the creek at high speed, spray dashing over them, white foam boiling behind them as Kit raced the engines like a madman. He was trying to frighten her, she knew that. Punishment for having the nerve to speak to Don without permission. He was treating her like a runaway slave, and her blood boiled to match the white water.

They were in the bay itself before Kit turned, bringing the boat around in a great circle, throttling back and heading into the creek with little of the madness left in him, it seemed. Charlotte was struggling to look calm and easy, as if she had enjoyed this wild ride, and deep down she had to admit that she *had* enjoyed it. It was the first time in her life that she had felt physical danger, and it was strangely exhilarating. Her clear skin was flushed and beautiful, her grey eyes sparkled with the experience.

'You damned well enjoyed that, didn't you?' Kit growled, his eyes running over her now that he did not need all his attention on the boat.

'Yes!' she said smugly. 'Thank you very much. Maybe we can do it again some day?'

He looked at her pert face, her tilted chin, and his lips quirked in a smile that was part admiration and part exasperation, but for the moment he said nothing.

She became aware that they were putting in to the bank, and her eyes were round with suspicion as Kit cut the engine and drifted close to the leafy overhang and under a tunnel of green branches.

'Why have we stopped?' She spun round and looked at him, at his tight expression.

'I want to talk to you without Essie spying and Don standing by to admire you!' he said briefly, his eyes on the bank, letting the boat bump gently against it.

'I don't want a lecture!'

She stood up and, before he could stop her, sprang out on to the bank.

To her extreme annoyance he ignored her, busying himself with tying the boat, his attention totally with his task, his hands lean and brown. She wished she could take her eyes off those hands, but she couldn't.

Kit finished tying the boat and then stepped easily out to stand beside her, his eyes on her downcast face. He stood quite still, watching her, saying nothing. He too was wearing shorts, and a blue and white sports shirt with horizontal stripes. He looked sporty, healthy and very, very American.

'I can see that you admire the shirt,' he said amusedly when she didn't speak, and refused to look at his face, but kept her eyes fixed on a point somewhere midway up his chest.

'I—yes, it looks French.'

'How's that?' He was laughing at her, she knew, and she glanced up to face him out, her eyes angry.

'I expect it's the latitudinal stripes!'

'The lati—what?' He grabbed her around her slim waist and pulled her hard against him, looking into her eyes and, just as she was sure that he was going to kiss her, he let her go. It was diabolical of him, almost as if he knew how she felt. They were both in shorts, and she had been shiveringly aware of his legs against hers, the rough rasp of his skin against her more tender silkiness. She dared not move an inch, in case she made herself more aware of him.

'The lecture is brief and to the point, Charlotte,' he said quietly. 'Don't encourage Don!'

'I was not encouraging him!' she snapped angrily. 'He's a friendly man! *You're* perfectly friendly with him!'

'He's not likely to want to kiss me!' Kit said wryly, and Charlotte's cheeks flooded with colour.

'He's not like that!' she raged quietly. 'He—he works for you!'

'He's a man!' Kit said tersely, adding scathingly, 'Didn't Gordon teach you anything about men?'

'No!' Charlotte rapped out before she could stop herself. 'I've found out from you!'

'Not enough!' he said softly. 'Before I can complete any lesson, you cry off!'

'I'm sorry!' she countered waspishly. 'I can't help it. It's disgust!'

And that was a mistake. She knew it as she saw his eyes blaze, and her quick movement to escape failed utterly. He pulled her harshly to him, moulding her to his taut body all in one smooth and furious movement.

'Oh!' Relief flooded through her, making her legs shake, her hands tremble. She had been wanting this since she had seen him this morning, her anger merely jealousy, and even that could not override the wild excitement of being with him.

He didn't move, his eyes blazing down into hers, reading her mind, and for a moment he held her away from him to allow his gaze to flare over her.

'All right, Charley,' he breathed. 'You like to live dangerously!'

His arms lashed around her and he pulled her back to the hard power of his body, his hand coming to cup her face.

'Once you called me deceitful. So are you deceitful, Charley!' he muttered thickly. 'We're two of a kind. You want me and you're pretending like hell that you don't—that's deceit too, my wild little wife. Underneath, you're all trembling and yearning.'

She opened her mouth to say that she was nothing of the kind, but it was far too late; his lips closed over hers and that was the end of any fight. She had been waiting for this for days, maybe all her life. His many crimes were forgotten, Veronica faded into the background and then out of sight as he slowly and hungrily devoured her.

'Kit!' Her protest was merely a low moan as he pulled her to the ground, to the crisp, sweet grass and turned her in his arms, trailed burning kisses over her neck and along her jawline, his fingers slipping open the buttons and her thin blouse and finding nothing but warm flesh beneath.

He had threatened her, she told herself. He had threatened reprisals that he would enjoy and she had not kept her tongue still. There was no gentleness in the fierce pressure of his mouth, and fear mixed with excitement shot through her. His weight held her to the ground and his hands roamed over her. He had kissed her and held her before but never like this, and a low moan came from her bruised lips as his fingers moved possessively and urgently on her breast.

'Don't! Please don't!' He heard her distress and eased away from her a little, his eyes blazing down at her.

'You're my wife, Charley,' he said softly. 'You were there when I married you, and you said, 'I do,' just like any other wife. Maybe you hated me as you said it, but you said it, Charley, and if I want you, you're mine. And, oh God, how I want you!'

His hands moved slowly now, caressingly, and he watched her face all the time, assessing her arousal, knowing exactly the moment when she gave up fighting, his eyes moving to the swollen evidence of her breasts before his mouth came down to draw one hard peak into its warmth.

'You've lost weight,' he muttered, raising his head and looking down at her body, and she could tell that even that knowledge excited him. 'You look younger than ever, all fragile and trembling.'

With every word he spoke his excitement was rising, and his eyes were hypnotising her.

'Those eyes have gone dark, Charley,' he murmured. 'Like two deep pools. You want me!'

'No!' she said frantically, coming to agitated life, but he drew her close, his lips hovering over hers.

'You're no better at lying than you ever were,' he taunted, his mouth covering hers, driving away the last possible reprieve. There was only the feeling of his arms tightly holding her, his kisses driving her to burning desire, his body moving urgently against her.

'Tell me you want me, Charley!' he ordered.

'No!' She gasped in delight as his hands swept seductively over her.

'Tell me!' he breathed into her mouth, his opened lips

catching hers as she sobbed,

'Yes! Yes!'

She had dreamed of him loving her, making love to her, and it had been gentle and slow, wonderful, but that was her own vivid imagination. This was Kit and this was real! He drew her into a raging storm of desire with no warning, his kisses drowning her, his caresses making her leap beneath his hands. He made no allowance whatever for her youth and inexperience. He wanted her and he wanted her now! She knew this Kit. She knew the power of him and the determination. Fright flared through her that swamped the magic. What was supposed to be the outcome of this? Was she to stay here for ever as a foil to cover for his meetings with Veronica Collins?

The enchantment, the sudden misery, were all swamped in red-hot rage, Don's unexpected attention to her and Kit's violent anger at it suggesting a plan of her own. Don't get mad, get even! She had heard that somewhere. She curled herself into his arms, her fingers lingering in his hair, her body moving against his.

'Honey?' Immediately he was gentle, easing off and wrapping his arms around her, lifting her away from the hard ground, closer to his body. 'I'm sorry if I scared you. I forgot for a second that you're such a little thing.' His voice was husky, his hands trembling, and Charlotte had to remind herself forcefully of her plans.

'I'm not!' She glanced up at him winsomely and a wry smile tilted his lips.

'You're like a beautiful little kitten, a sexy little kitten. It's hard to keep my hands off you, Charley.'

With a low groan, he lowered his head to the throbbing peak of her breast, and waves of delight shot through her. For a second, a shameful, revealing second, her fingers threaded through his hair, welcoming this intimate invasion, and then she remembered just why she was Kit's wife, remembered his iniquity.

'No, Kit!' She pushed him away and he raised his head, looking at her with dazed eyes.

'Charley?' He didn't seem to realise that it was just not possible to have everything he wanted. So typically male! Her expression must have given her away and his eyes suddenly focused, piercingly blue, narrowed and understanding. 'I could take you here and now, Charley!' he grated.

'I don't doubt it,' she whispered, her eyes firmly closed as she realised how dangerous this state of affairs could become. 'But afterwards things would be slightly different between us. I wouldn't be quite so easy to dismiss when my usefulness was over; you'd have one of those messy battles on your hands that you despair of and I'd really hate you.' She could feel growing tension in his body, no longer a sexual tension. He was simmering with fury, his eyes would be burning her. 'You were the one who set up the ground rules,' she pointed out. 'You can't alter things now. If I had even suspected that this sort of thing would happen, I wouldn't be here, not even for Uncle Joe.'

'Open your eyes!' he snapped, so harshly that she obeyed instantly, her eyes wide as she looked at him.

'You may not be the worst liar in the whole world,' he growled, 'but you run a very close second. What's eating you, Charley?'

'Only my aversion to this kind of thing! You're stronger than I am and there's not much I can do about it, but I can certainly tell you. I'm telling you!' She looked away, blushingly aware that she was still half naked, and he grunted in a furious manner, fastening her blouse, his eyes on her tight breasts until the last button was closed.

'OK, Charlotte!' he grated, standing and hauling her to her feet. 'I'll overlook the way you respond to me. I'll bear your comments in mind. But a word of warning—don't provoke me too far. Better keep those long legs well covered; you're too tempting by half!'

After lunch he announced coldly that he had to fly out and wouldn't be back until the day of the party. He handed her a list of guests and left. She didn't dare to question him at the moment, so she was at the mercy of Essie, which turned out to be a good thing. They planned the party together and established a code for future co-operation in the house. Clearly, Essie wanted her to be Mrs Landor and to take some sort of charge. She did; it all fitted in with her plan of getting even. Kit was hardly likely to feel any sting if she merely moped about feeling sorry for herself.

CHAPTER NINE

TO CHARLOTTE'S amazement, Veronica called round to see her.

'I'm afraid that Kit isn't here,' Charlotte said, the remark slipping out coolly before she could stop it.

'Oh, I know that, Charlotte. In fact, if he had been here then I wouldn't have come at all. People do talk, you know, and in spite of the distances from one estate to another, they all seem to know each other's business!'

She wasn't trying really hard, Charlotte thought. This was outright attack, neatly parcelled up with a smile. She chose to misunderstand, looking as close to stupid as she could manage.

'I came to see whether or not you fancied going to Baltimore,' Veronica added brightly after a close look at her. 'I'm definitely going. I want a new dress for this party of yours, and I can't get one around here. It would be a good thing to take you to see Baltimore. You could get a dress for yourself, thought I expect that you've got plenty of evening dresses?'

Yes, Charlotte thought. There were still three that she had never worn, one of which figured very largely in her future plans. Kit had arranged for her to have a bank account and credit cards, but she had no intention of being any further in his debt.

'I've got plenty to wear, Veronica, and I can't really spare the time. Kit had to go away and I've got the party to arrange.'

'You can leave that safely to Essie,' Veronica said

sharply. 'She knows the sort of thing that's expected. Nothing varies here. There's a good deal of tradition attached to things that take place at Markland. Kit will be furious if you alter things.'

Until that moment, she had not had the slightest intention of doing so; now though, it was sheer necessity.

'I'm sure that Essie will guide me,' she said quietly, adding with a secret smile, 'and Kit never gets furious with me, although I have seen him in rages with other people. If I make any mistakes, he'll only laugh. He's so good to me!' she crooned.

Veronica rose to go, her face no longer scathing, and Charlotte marked up one point to herself.

'I'll looked forward to the party, then. I do admire your courage, Charlotte.'

And hate me to your back teeth, Charlotte added to herself. Aloud she said, 'Oh, I don't have much. Kit takes care of me.' Veronica left at that.

She had plenty of ideas for the party, all of them a great surprise to Essie.

'We always do things the same way,' she said worriedly, her hands busy with pastry.

'Then now is a good time for a change!' Charlotte insisted firmly. 'Time to give things a good jolt!'

'Mr Kit ain't goin' to like this!' Essie grumbled, and Charlotte put her foot down firmly and finally.

'Mr Landor left me to arrange the party. I'll arrange it! First of all, we'll have it as fancy dress affair.'

'Fancy dress! What sort of a party is that?' Essie glowered at her like Kit, and Charlotte got ready to battle. She had some very wicked plans, and Essie was not going to stop her.

'A fancy dress party is where you have fancy dress,'

Don Segal pointed out, walking into the kitchen at that moment.

'Well, I know that!' Essie turned her annoyance on him and Charlotte put a stop to that at once.

'Good! So long as you understand. Now, we'll have lights under the trees,' she added like a jolly and enthusiastic Girl Guide mistress. 'We could dance out there, too, if we could rig up some sort of a floor.'

'That's easy enough done,' Don said from his perch on the edge of the kitchen table before Essie could gather her breath for another outraged bellow. He had taken to hanging around happily when Charlotte was there, and he added to her enthusiasm. 'There's a firm who will come out and lay a temporary floor in two shakes. They'll put up a marquee, too.'

'No marquee!' Charlotte ordered. 'Just the floor and the lights!'

'Well, did Mr Kit—I mean—did you have dancing in mind when you thought of the party, Miss Charlotte?' Essie asked, changing horses in mid-stream.

'No, but I think it would be nice, and if we have it outside then it will take a little strain off the household arrangements.'

'That's true!' Essie said firmly, giving the idea her approval.

'There a five-piece band in town,' Don suggested helpfully.

'Oh, Don! Could you arrange it and the floor? And ask them if they can supply the lights when they bring the floor. It will save us having to do it.'

'I'm all for that!' Essie nodded. 'Forecast's good for the whole month, and last night was as warm as could be!'

'Well then, Don? Can we leave all that to you?' Charlotte said getting her office manner back for a few seconds.

'Sure, Mrs Landor. I'll get at it right away!' He turned to leave, but Charlotte stopped him as an idea occurred to her.

'Oh, Don! We want the floor at the side of the house. The side away from the helicopter pad. We'll give Mr Landor a surprise on the night.'

'Yes, ma'am!' He went off grinning, and Essie added her thoughts in a low mutter.

'I sure hope it ain't a shock that he gets. That man can be awkward, and we never had no tree lights here before!'

'There's a first time for everything!' Charlotte said firmly, walking off before her office manner could desert her. There was a first time for being downright nasty and deceitful too, not to say spiteful, but she was determined to do it!

Brett had been happy to accept the invitation when she had phoned him, and when he flew in on Saturday afternoon she ran across the lawn to meet him. His face lit up with pleasure and she knew that she had captured at least *his* heart. Her own heart leapt as she saw Kit climb out, too, but she allowed herself to be bear-hugged by his grandfather and merely smiled briefly at him.

'How's my new granddaughter?' Brett overwhelmed her and began to lead her to the house, with no thought of her going to her husband.

'Too busy to greet her husband by the look of it!' Kit bit out sharply, but as she turned to go to him Brett caught her around the waist and ploughed on with a heavy disregard for anyone else.

'You get to see her all the time. I only just discovered her! Don't be jealous, boy!'

It quite suited Charlotte, and obviously Brett was quite used to having his own way and even tried to bulldoze Kit when the chance arose. She was swept into the house on Brett's enthusiasm.

It was only later, as she ran up to her room, that Kit had the chance to take her to task.

'Remember me?' He was standing in her room, the door slamming behind him before she could think, and his expression was complete aggression.

'I didn't get the chance to ask you how your trip went . . .' she began, fading out altogether as he advanced on her furiously.

'Ask me now!' he rasped, towering over her. 'But first, let me show you what will happen every time you ignore me in public!'

He grasped her arms, pulling her forward, ignoring her cry of outrage.

'Brett takes second place in this house!' he grated. 'And second place in your life! You're married to me, not to the chairman of Sanford Petrochemicals, and don't forget it again.'

He cupped her face, his fingers spearing into her thick hair, his mouth catching hers in a furiously angry kiss that robbed her of breath. Her struggles were futile and he did not let her go until he was quite ready. He stared down at her with hard blue eyes, his hands still gripping her tightly.

'Well, hello, Charlotte!' he said ironically, and she closed her eyes to hide the sudden tears.

She was filled with a trembling desire to be close to him, longing for him to love her, his hard and unforgiving kiss hurting inside as it had not hurt her physically. She had missed him so much, but her future existence could not depend on that. She would always be in this state if she didn't act, force him to send her away.

It wasn't just a matter of getting even, it was a matter of survival. Kit liked things as they were, Veronica included. She intended to change everything, to really interfere with his life, and the party was just the first step. She couldn't let things stay as they were.

'I hate you, Kit!' she whispered huskily, knowing that she did not at all.

'Open your eyes and say that again!' he dared her, and she slowly opened her eyes, the clear grey pools filled with tears that sparkled on her lashes, partly anger, partly sheer misery.

For a second they looked at each other, and then he folded her into his arms, his head bending as his lips found hers again.

'Why, Charley! You missed me!' he said, his words softly derisive against her mouth, his lips brushing back and forth across hers. 'Are you going to tell me that you wanted me to come home? Are you, Charley?'

His lips teased hers unbearably, and his hands moved over her back and then under the soft material of her shirt to caress her warm flesh and arch her against him.

'Tell me, Charley!' he ordered in an insistent voice, his hands around her, his thumbs brushing the rise of her breasts.

'I missed you!' she murmured. 'I missed you, Kit!'

He waited no longer, his mouth claiming hers in a long, deep kiss that was heaven itself, and she stopped pretending immediately, allowing herself to be drawn into the magic, her arms winding around his neck, her lips opening invitingly beneath his. She told herself that it was because she knew better than to tackle him head on, but her body asked her just who she was fooling.

His hands roamed over her as the kiss deepened, and she heard her own little moans, but they seemed to be coming from a very long way away. His body hardened against her at the sound of them, and he tightened her to him with a passion that took her remaining breath away, making her cry out and pull away, fearful of allowing this to go too far.

'Because you're scared or because you don't want to, Charley?' he asked thickly, raising his head and staring down at her. His own breathing was none too steady, and she knew that he had been on the very edge of losing control.

'Miss Charlotte?' There was a knock on the door, and Essie's voice called to her as Kit let her go with obvious reluctance.

'That's a question that I'm going to ask again, Charley,' he murmured as he moved away. 'You'd better be sorting out your answer!'

Suddenly she knew that it would be hard to fight Kit, because everybody was on his side, including herself.

It was a feeling that lingered. Through the rest of the day she tried to avoid Kit's eyes, so shy that she felt unable to speak to him, and he clearly misunderstood because his temper hovered on the brink of explosion, only the presence of Brett keeping him silent. Even so, she never had the opportunity to be alone with his grandfather, because wherever she went Kit was only one step behind her, until it really began to look as if he objected to her speaking to Brett at all.

And she was in a state of nervous tension, too, about her plans for the evening. The invitations had gone out in good time, invitations for a fancy dress party, the men to wear ordinary evening dress, all perfectly normal. It was no worry. What was worrying was the outcome of her later telephone calls, and she was beginning to wonder now if spite was a good thing, after all. She had phoned every woman, telling them exactly what kind of a fancy dress party this was to be, something in keeping with the house, a very old ballgown, fans, they knew the kind of thing and would they please keep it strictly secret, it was a surprise for her husband. Naturally they had been intrigued and delighted, and Charlotte knew that they could well afford to deck themselves out in old-fashioned finery.

She had not phoned Veronica, although the invitation had been exactly like the others. She intended to do her own killing of two birds with one stone. This would be a grand party—spectacular—and she intended to see to it that Veronica stood out clearly. Maybe she would come as a witch! If Kit wanted Veronica in the background, then he was not getting it tonight. She knew he would be furious. If Veronica came dressed differently, wherever she went eyes would be on her, and if Kit wanted to be with her then he would also take the limelight. Charlotte knew that it would probably be the last straw. She could see him packing her off back to England at once.

She went to get ready for the party, and by now the floor, the band and the lights in the trees were all arranged. Kit seemed not to have realised that there was anything at all different. He was too annoyed to give a thought to anything else. Later he would explode, but for now the evening was in her own hands, if she could keep her nerve. Perhaps he would not send her away at once, but little by little she would annoy him until he did. It was all a matter of water on a stone, and she would play so innocent. He could hardly blame her for trying, and her bargain would not be broken if Kit simply got fed up with her. Her uncle would be safe.

Essie, too, held her tongue. She didn't know of course about the little final touch of the telephone calls, but she did know that things would be very different tonight, the party on a much larger scale than Kit had ever bothered with before. Her eyes slid to Charlotte from time to time in a sort of uneasy conspiracy but, probably for the first time in her life, she said nothing.

The white dress, one that she had bought in London, was almost a crinoline, riding out around her on wide skirts, and she pulled the top down until her shoulders were bare. She wore the diamonds that Kit had given her, and on an impulse she made her hair into ringlets that framed her face and fell in shining cascades beside her slender neck. Shades of Scarlett O'Hara! It took a long time, longer than she had expected, and she heard Kit coming before she was quite ready.

'Charlotte! They'll be here soon!' he called out as he came into the room, but she was already locked in the bathroom, hiding behind the door like a criminal, a little scared now at her plotting.

'I'll be there!'

'Then hurry up!' he rasped, going out and slamming the door. 'Don't come down sulking!'

Sulking? She had thought that she had sounded quite merry. A rising temper banished guilt and she marched out, putting the diamond ear-rings on and the diamanté clasp for good measure. Glittering with diamonds and rage, she went out of her room, her face flushing with further annoyance to see Essie peering over the banisters, watching guests arrive, looking like a criminal associate.

'Mercy, Miss Charlotte! I thought for one minute that you were a ghost!' Essie spun round, her hand clutching her heart as Charlotte moved forward.

'I'm not that pale!' Charlotte snapped, and Essie looked at her admiringly.

'It's not that! You look lovely, like a lady from long ago. I thought that we'd got ourselves haunted! Not that we haven't got enough without ghosts,' she added darkly. 'Mr Kit will know now what's been done!'

She suddenly smiled proudly, before Charlotte could

explode.

'This is the grandest party we've had for years! Those ladies coming in now looking good enough to eat, and all that big buffet you decided on. I've nothing to do at all now. The clearing can wait until tomorrow when those girls you hired get to it. Biggest and easiest thing I've done!' she announced gleefully, her face falling when music began. 'That band's startin'! Mr Kit will know now!'

She hurried off and Charlotte went forward to face the music in more ways than one. Damn Mr Kit! He had said that she was the boss-lady. Tonight she would show him how much!'

The great, sweeping staircase could not have been a better background for an entrance. There were plenty of people still milling around in the huge, shining hall, and Kit was at the door greeting new arrivals. It was the sudden silence and the fact that the newcomers were not looking at him that drew Kit's attention to her, and she knew that he would be still stunned by the appearance of so many 'southern belles'.

He must have been, because when his eyes met hers they were dazed, almost uncomprehending. He walked forward to meet her, waiting at the foot of the stairs, taking her hand as soon as she was within reach.

'A band has arrived,' he said quietly, so that only Charlotte could hear.

'Good! I expected them. We'll be dancing under the trees. There are lights there and a good floor!' She said it with a defiant air that had the dazed look growing slowly across the whole of his tanned face.

If this much had stunned him into silence, what would he say when Veronica arrived on her broomstick?

'Save the first dance for me, Charley,' he said softly. 'I—I think we'd better talk.'

She had to admit that that alarmed her, that and his suddenly softened attitude. Was it the lull before the storm, or the stalking of the prey? His hand was warm and not at all frightening, though, and she was riding a high of achievement, her smile glittering to match the diamonds as he led her forward, keeping her hand in his.

It couldn't have been better; Veronica and Eric arrived at that moment, Veronica stopping in the doorway as if she had been struck a blow.

'Glad to see you arrived on time, Eric!' Kit said with a wide smile. 'There's to be a few changes tonight. Charley's been left in charge and there's a band and tree lights. I can't wait to see Brett queuing to get a dance with her.'

'He can get behind me!' Eric laughed. 'I feel as if I should have arrived in a horse-drawn carriage! Isn't she something?' He bowed and kissed Charlotte's hand, getting into the swing of things and Kit smiled tightly.

'Isn't she, though?' he murmured. His eyes met Veronica's. 'Didn't you know it was fancy dress?'

'Oh, she knew!' Eric answered before Veronica could get a word out, although Charlotte wondered if Veronica would ever be able to speak again, she was so angry. 'She thought that fancy dress was a bit beneath her dignity, didn't you, darling?' he asked with a grin of wry amusement. 'Didn't fancy coming as the Sugar Plum Fairy. How odd,' he added, his nice face puzzled. 'Every lady in a crinoline. They usually go out of the way to out-do each other in things like this. You'd think they'd been conspiring.'

'You would!' Kit said curtly, his hand on Charlotte's hard and biting.

Veronica was smiling in a strained manner, her eyes like ice as she met Charlotte's welcoming smile.

'You look very striking, Charlotte. Just what the

house needs!'

'Thank you,' Charlotte murmured. 'It's a good thing that I had this dress with me.'

Kit looked thoughtfully at them both, and then swept her out on to the steps to greet more guests.

'Kit, about the party . . .' she began, her nerve suddenly deserting her, but his arm came tightly around her narrow waist and he gave her a sort of threatening squeeze.

'Not now, sweetheart,' he said softly, his whole attitude hostility, his smile bright and cheerful as new guests arrived. 'Later. I think that you and I will have to have a good talk when everybody's gone home.' He gave a sudden harsh laugh. 'Tree lights and an outside dance-floor. I wonder what have happened if it had rained?'

'Essie said that it wouldn't!' she informed him tartly, her cheeks now flushed with the desire to battle openly.

'That being the case, then, it wouldn't dare!' Kit said wryly. 'Come on, let's get inside. There are about sixty people in there just dying to get a look at you.'

'Don't forget that they'll be watching you, too!' she said smartly.

He bent and kissed her cheek for the benefit of Brett who was hovering around waiting.

'You look like a dream, Charley!' he breathed against her ear. 'Nobody is going to notice me!'

It was all a huge success and Veronica kept her distance, talking animatedly to other people whenever Eric came to talk to them. Charlotte was furious. She seemed to spend most of the evening in Kit's arms as he claimed one dance after another. Her plan had backfired on a grand scale, and Kit seemed to be pleased as punch, knowing her irritation and no doubt guessing the cause.

'I'm having so much fun!' she confided bitterly, and he tightened his hold on her warmly.

'So you should be, Charley!' he said derisively. 'You deserve it!'

'Do you like the party?' she asked, getting off the subject of just deserts very quickly. Every move that Kit made seemed to ring bells inside her, and she had to work really hard to stop herself from gazing at him all the time. It was trickier than she had thought, to maintain irritation and be held so close to him. She hadn't banked on this. She had expected him to go straight to Veronica, but obviously he was not so foolish.

'Wonderful! I love to see all these folks paying court to Brett. It's good for his ego. He'll be here a lot more often now that you're here. He likes to pay court to you!'

'Would you want him here more often?' she said in surprise, forgetting her annoyance and her other problem.

'I would!' He looked down at her. 'Don't be fooled by our attitude. We care about each other. Brett brought me up after my folks died. We had nobody but each other.'

'I'm sorry,' Charlotte said, softly sympathetic, and he smiled quizzically.

'Don't be. I've got you now, Charley!'

She looked up at him, startled and worried by his suddenly determined tone. What could he mean? He was not looking at her, however, and the moment passed as Brett finally made his displeasure felt and demanded to be allowed a dance.

There was great enthusiasm for the party, and people lingered as long as they could, coming at last to thank both of them for a great time.

'Can we have a dress-up party again soon, Kit?' one young lady asked as she left with her parents and her boyfriend. 'Dressing up is so great for this house!'

'You'll have to check that out with Charlotte,' Kit

laughed. 'All this is nothing to do with me!'

'Can we, Charlotte?' she asked excitedly.

'When I've got my breath back!' Charlotte smiled, feeling really like a successful hostess and an utterly failed conspirator. Everybody was happy except her!

She caught Veronica's eye and a shiver went over her. Veronica was not happy! She had not heard the end of Veronica, in spite of her attempt to get the better of her.

She told Brett that she was tired, and he saw nothing wrong with that.

'You've got a great girl here, Kit!' Brett averred, his arm coming around her. 'A beautifully planned party! Great theme! It would have done justice to a hostess of twice her age or more!'

'She's smart for her age!' Kit agreed sardonically, and Charlotte glared at him secretly. Not smart enough, apparently. He was supposed to have been seen with Veronica, been driven out into the open. Instead he had stayed with her, ruined her plans and made her heart race all evening. She was pretty close to sulking, after all, as she went to bed.

She threw off the jewellery and pulled her hair free, admitting that she felt childishly angry. Everything had backfired. The party had been a great success, one that would be talked over for ages. Kit had out-foxed her with ease, and now everyone would be saying how devoted he was to his nice new wife.

He walked in without knocking, just as she was trying to unzip her dress, and she spun round angrily.

'Will you get out?'

'We were going to talk,' he said with a reasonable air that warned of danger.

'I don't want to talk!' She began to brush her hair, unable to think of anything else to do, and he lingered by the door, watching.

'Tonight was a great success, Charley,' he said softly. 'I can't think why you're so angry about it. Did something go wrong, then?'

'Not a thing! When I organise something, it gets done properly!' she snapped.

'Then why so irritated? I thought it was great, and so did Brett. It's just about the best party we've had, and no Essie about to get underfoot—you even organised her out of it. Of course, Veronica didn't come as a teddy bear. That spoiled your evening a bit, didn't it? Never mind, better luck next time.'

'I shan't bother again!' Charlotte flared, quite forgetting to be silent. 'But sooner or later, somebody is going to notice how much time you spend with her, then this will all be pointless. Then I'll be free!'

'I'm doing this for Eric!' he said quietly. 'I told you that. Where's your trust, Charley?'

'Don't you dare mention that word to me!' Charlotte shouted, lowering her voice as she realised that Brett was staying. 'There's been nothing to trust since I first met you. And in any case, you nearly killed me when I talked nicely to Don! You took that boat out like a madman!' You've got no trust in me! We're supposed to be both part of the same bargain.'

She turned away angrily, alarmed when he came to stand behind her.

'As far as I'm concerned,' he said quietly, 'the evening was an unqualified success. As to Don, that was pure green-eyed jealousy. I want you myself and I'm not the calm kind of person who stands smiling while somebody else takes what I want.'

'You—you can't say that!' Charlotte whispered.

Every part of her seemed to be flooding with heat, and she was sure that even her back and shoulders were blushingly hot.

'I just did. I've said it before. You know I want you, Charley. Hell! I can't keep my hands off you!' he added angrily.

'This is a bargain!' Charlotte reminded him quickly, swinging round to face him. 'I'm only here to be—be a hostage for my uncle!'

'Then you can consider the bargain to be off,' he said softly, his eyes seriously on hers.

'What are you going to do to Uncle Joe?' she whispered, her eyes wide, her whole being shaken. She didn't know why he was saying this. Had her plan succeeded, after all? A great wave of sadness and regret clouded her eyes, and he went on looking at her with that serious look that made her legs tremble.

'I'm doing nothing to Joe,' he asured her quietly. 'Joe's related to me, don't forget.'

'He's not—he . . .'

'I married his niece,' Kit reminded her softly. They went on looking at each other in silence until he reached out and drew her to him, turning her and drawing her back against his hard body, his lips brushing her shoulders. 'Sleep with me, Charley!' he said deeply. 'I want you!'

She shook her head frantically, her mind adding up the cost of such magic, but his lips continued their devastating caresses over her shoulders and nape, his hands tightly possessive on her arms, and the room began its old familiar spinning.

'I won't! I—I can't!' she whispered wildly, but he merely pulled her closer, blending her to him, forcing hard reality into the distance.

'You're my wife, Charley,' he murmured.

'I—I'm not! Not really!' she said shakily. She could feel the hammering of his heart right through her, and she had to fight away the great surge of joy that came when she realised how great a power she had over him at this moment, a woman's power as old as Eve.

'I want to make it real,' he muttered, his breathing heavy. 'I want you to stay here. Damn it, Charley! I've got used to you! I'm used to battling with you, taking care of you, kissing you! I can't stop kising you! Surely you've noticed that?'

He sank his face into her hair and then, as if unable to resist it, his lips trailed down her spine, the silken rasp of his skin sending shivers of delight through her. His hands tightened, his whole body shuddering against hers, and Charlotte cried out softly as he moved with seductive slowness to unzip the lovely dress and slide his hands urgently inside to cup her breasts.

'You—you can't!' It was an enslaved protest and she knew that herself, not doubting at all that Kit heard it.

'We both know that I'm going to,' he said vibrantly.

He turned her, sliding the dress away, leaving her in just the lacy half-slip, and colour raced across his cheekbones as he looked at her, his hands reaching out unhurriedly to touch the sharp rose-tinted peaks, knowing that however slow his reaching, she would not turn away. She closed her eyes, every feeling inflamed, her body tense with suppressed rapture, shaking uncontrollably as he spanned her waist with fierce hands, his head bending to take one uptilted breast into the warmth of his mouth with punishing urgency.

Her softly frenzied cries stopped him and he pulled her violently to him, his lips hovering over hers.

'Marry me, Charley!' he begged vibrantly. 'Tonight! Now!'

And Charlotte was beyond any kind of speech. Somewhere at the very back of her mind, danger bells rang, a little voice asking her how she had come from defiant anger to this. But she was too bewitched to resist this seduction, too enslaved to fight her way out of the enchantment. Mutely, her lips searched for Kit's and he claimed them with a feverish demand that sent fierce shafts of excitement through her entire being.

Hunger that had been growing for days exploded inside her, and she responded with a passion that seemed to drive him wild. The coaxing hands became insistent and burning as her remaining flimsy garments were removed, and Charlotte clung to him, knowing that she would fall if the tight arm around her was removed.

She was responding with all the ardency of her nature, holding nothing back in her love for him, and her passion had driven him beyond reason. He was shaking with the intensity of this, as if her willing response was a complete surprise, more than he had thought, and his kiss deepened to an almost aggressive act of possession.

'Charley!' he breathed unsteadily, lifting his lips just a fraction away from hers, his warm breath against her mouth. 'You've thrown every last choice away. I want you now.'

With a desperate cry, Charlotte moved back to the hard warmth of him, her lips anxious against the smooth rasp of his cheeks, and his body surged with desire as he pulled her crushingly to him, his mouth opening over hers and taking everything that she offered.

His hand held her head to his, his mouth draining her, leaving her trembling and burning, her breath sobs in her throat as he removed his own clothes with movements that were almost violent, before pulling her to the hard demand of his body.

'Kit!' There was panic in her voice as he tightened her to him, but he didn't seem to hear, his own driving need the only thing in his mind as, with a murmur of frustration, he pulled her to the bed.

'We can't do this!' Belatedly she struggled, the future suddenly bleak in her mind, but he grasped her chin, forcing her mouth open, his kisses lengthening, deepening until her protests were drowned, going down into the velvet vortex with her.

In some distant world she could feel the caresses that were driving her to move ardently against him. Far away she could hear his voice murmuring her name, and she knew that she was driving him on to this, forcing all thoughts of her innocence out of his mind.

'Now, Charley,' he muttered thickly, his fondling hands moving to lift her. 'You're coming with me!'

Inside she was burning, waves of fire flooding her lethargic limbs, caution a thing of the past. Her body gloried in the power of his, no fright in her. His eyes, vividly blue, filled her whole world, the burning need in them bringing back the knowledge of her power over this hard, self-sufficient man.

He drew her into a blaze of fire, her cry panic-stricken when he possessed her, pain shooting through her limbs at the power of it, and then honeyed sweetness that exploded into a million stars bringing a wild cry to her lips that seemed to come from light years away.

'Charley!' he gasped her name, and then the whole world rocked and tilted as he clasped her convulsively to him, their bodies throbbing together.

She drifted from the clouds reluctantly, wanting to be back there, tears escaping from the corners of her closed eyes. For minutes, or hours, she could not tell which, she had been alone in the world with Kit, and now they were back, back where people could intrude, back where Veronica could try to claim him again, back where his arms could reach for someone else.

'Charley.' He spoke her name softly and she opened

her eyes with reluctance, the tears growing into heart-rending sobs as she turned away from him, knowing now how easy it was for a man to subdue a woman; her anger and defiance had been so puny in face of this. She felt ill with the knowledge of what had happened, of what her future would become now, and she leapt wildly from the bed, frantically seeking the bathroom, slamming the door and bolting it before Kit could reach her. She was sure he would be gone when she ventured out finally. But he simply waited, lifting her into his arms and walking to the bed, placing her under the cool sheets. Reaction was setting in rapidly now, and exhaustion, but she was grateful when Kit put out the lights and slid into bed beside her, pulling her into his arms almost gently, his hands soothing her as she drifted into a deep, dreamless sleep.

CHAPTER TEN

WHEN Charlotte awoke in the morning, the cloud of misery was still around her. She had no memory of having drifted off to sleep, but she remembered that in the night he had lifted her into his arms, pulling her to his warmth, soothing away her unhappy sounds until she sighed and went to sleep again.

He was dressing, white jeans close against his strong legs, his shirt a soft, dark blue just being pulled over his head, and she watched him unashamedly, her face flushed and her eyes dreamy as they ran over him.

'Dreaming, Charley?'

He was watching her too, his eyes narrowed and blue on her face, and she blushed furiously to have been caught watching him, to be here as he dressed. Memories of the previous night flooded through her, the passion that had gripped them both, his fierce determination to own her. What had brought that on? Anger? Frustration that Veronica was out of his reach that night?

His words came back to her, too. He was breaking the agreement, keeping her here. He would be keeping Veronica here, too. A mixture of emotions filled her, colouring her expression. She wanted to wake like this each day, knowing that she had spent the night in Kit's arms, but it would only be when Veronica was unavailable.

'Charley?'

For a second he looked impatient with her, or so it

171

seemed to her agitated mind, and she avoided his eyes, lying there like a mouse. With an exasperated sigh he sank to the bed beside her, sitting still for a moment before lifting her into his arms.

'Charley, about last night . . .'

'I'd rather not talk about it,' she managed through stiff lips, a shudder running through her when she remembered how she had felt close to him, belonging to him. Obviously he mistook the reason for it.

'Charley!' he murmured, his hands stroking her hair back and then pulling her head to his shoulder, his attitude strangely protective. 'We must talk about it!'

'No!' She stiffened in his arms. She wanted no explanations. If he was going to tell her now that it had been frustration and that he was sorry, offer her some recompense, then she didn't want to know!

He jerked her head up angrily, staring at her for a second, his voice harsh when she closed her eyes tightly, her whole body stiff and unyielding.

'I'm not slow at getting messages!' he rasped. 'I know I hurt you, but . . .' He suddenly stood, leaving her to dive back under the sheets.

'If you get up and put some jeans on, I'll take you out on the launch,' he offered tightly. 'Let's not forget that we have a visitor today!' He stopped at the door, his irritated gaze flaring over her as she sat with the sheets pulled up to her chin, her eyes two silvery pools of distress. 'We'll take Brett with us,' he added caustically. 'That way you'll be safe enough, I guess!'

Kit brought the launch up to the landing-stage from further along the creek, and with a lunch packed by Essie they went out for the day, intending to head for the wider waters of Chesapeake Bay. Charlotte was glad in many ways that Brett was with them. She was still filled with a deep shyness about last night, still puzzled and worried, her eyes unable to meet Kit's, unable to keep away from him when he was not looking.

She was not glad however, when, just as they were ready to go, Veronica and Eric arrived, already dressed for the water, Veronica in a silky-looking sports outfit that made Charlotte's blue jeans look like working clothes.

'Just in time!' Kit called, his eyes on Veronica, and in spite of Brett's ferocious look they came, Eric blithely unaware of any atmosphere at all. It was how Kit had planned to spend his day: the security of numbers around him, Veronica well within his sight. Charlotte saw Brett watching her with a frown as she in her turn had been watching Veronica. Brett knew. The only small comfort was that he certainly did not approve.

Even the way that Veronica sat herself down on the deck was possessive, familiar, and although Kit seemed to be ignoring her there was a smug expression on Veronica's face that finally drove away the last tingles of delight from Charlotte. Nothing remained of last night's magic now, but regret and loneliness.

Still, there was Brett, and he set out to spoil her with a great determination. As for Kit, he handled the launch and spent a great deal of time talking to Eric.

They anchored close to a tree-covered island for lunch, sitting out on the sunny deck to eat.

'Like old times, eh, Kit?' Brett said heavily after a while. 'Time was when you and Eric spent every spare minute on the water.'

'We were best friends!' Kit said with a smile at Eric. 'Right from the first.'

'Hope we still are!' Eric said with a laugh that contained some small element of doubt.

'Friends, yes,' Kit said slowly, his eyes on Charlotte as he walked over and sat close to her. 'Best friends, now

. . . I don't know. I really think that Charley is my best friend.'

'Wives don't count!' Veronica put in with a sharp laugh, her eyes filled with keen interest.

'Charley does!' Kit said softly, his arm coming around Charlotte's neck, his wrist tilting her chin. 'I've always been Charley's friend.'

She found herself looking into his eyes, her own eyes puzzled, trying to work out how this would be an advantage to him. For a second, a muscle jerked at the side of his mouth, and then he covered her startled lips with his, kissing her in front of everyone. For Eric's benefit—that was all it was! Tears sparkled deep in her eyes, and Kit's gaze narrowed as he looked down at her.

Brett looked comfortably pleased, but the expression on Veronica's face was thoughtful. Far from making her stay in her place, the kiss and the words that had accompanied it seemed to make her bold.

'I was wondering if you still have that apartment in Galveston, Kit?'

'Sure, I never bother with it now, though. One of these days I'm going to get rid of it,' Kit said with little interest, his arm tightening around Charlotte when she surreptitiously tried to move away.

'I always liked it,' Veronica said with a reminiscent smile. 'Can I borrow it for a night or two soon? I'm going to go down there to see my aunt, and wild horses wouldn't make me stay with her.'

'Any time,' Kit said easily. 'Just let me know.'

'Oh, I will!' Veronica smiled at him widely, and this time Charlotte saw Eric's face cloud with anger, an anger that to her surprise did not appear to be directed at Kit at all.

It dawned on her that she was really a stranger here, an outsider. She even felt an embarrassment at the way she had taken so much to Brett. She felt as if she had pushed her way into his affections. The sobering thoughts silenced her, and the fact did not escape the sharp eyes of Veronica. Kit too moved away from her, his cool face evidence enough that he found her annoying.

Brett stayed on. There were business interests to attend to in Baltimore, and while he was here he decided to take action about them. Kit too was needed, and the evening saw them hard at work in Kit's study, Brett's growls of anger frequently heard as he and Kit argued things out. Charlotte felt very much an outsider and she wandered up to bed early, still not asleep when Kit came up very late.

She ignored his quiet tap on her door, disappointment and relief wildly mixed up inside her when he walked away to his own room without repeating that particular experiment. They must have left early, because when she got up next morning they were already gone. Kit had not even asked her if she would like a day out in the city she had never seen.

It was well into the afternoon when Veronica arrived, a certain smugness about her that made Charlotte's heart sink.

'There's nobody here,' Charlotte observed tensely when they were settled with coffee and Essie had gone from the room with a warning look at Charlotte.

'I didn't expect there to be,' Veronica announced, crossing her elegant legs and smiling widely. 'You're here, though. I thought it was about time that we had everything out into the open. I could see that you didn't miss the little signals that Kit and I gave each other yesterday. I'm going to Kit's apartment in Galveston in a couple of days, and you know really, don't you, that Kit will diappear at about the same time? That apartment is so damned useful!' she finished with a sigh of contentment.

'It doesn't seem to be very useful to him,' Charlotte said tightly, a little tired of the sly innuendo. 'He told me that he never stays there himself now!'

'But he's going to be away so often! His job takes him everywhere! How can you possibly tell where he stays?' Veronica asked with raised brows, a small and satisfied smile edging her lips.

'Just say exactly what you mean to say!' Charlotte snapped, tired by this kind of thing and ready to throw Veronica out without much more ado, even if Kit killed her for it.

'Oh, be your age!' The gloves, it appeared, were off at last, and the beautiful face was twisted in annoyance. 'How do you expect to hang on to a man like Kit Landor? He's not likely to be satisfied with friendship for very long.'

'I'm a little more than a friend,' Charlotte said heatedly. 'I'm his wife!'

'Well, you certainly don't look it! Kit and I have been closer than friends for years, and even though he's wild with me for marrying Eric, he still feels the same. I only married Eric to spite him after a quarrel. You know how he can be so awkward.'

'He's never awkward with me,' Charlotte lied, hanging on grimly to her last grain of happiness.

'Well, why should he be? After all, you're not really his wife. He married you to cover up the fact that we still see each other, and I know his code of honour, he'll never touch you really. He'll give you a great allowance and send you about your business!'

'I think not,' Charlotte said angrily. 'If you're suggesting that there could be an annulment, then forget it! I'm Kit's wife! For all I know I might be pregnant right at this moment!'

'You're lying!' Veronica sprang to her feet, her tanned face white. 'Kit would never . . .'

'I'm his wife and I'm a permanent part of his life,' Charlotte said firmly, rising to her own feet and going to open the door. 'Think it over as you drive off.'

'There's nothing to think over!' Veronica said bitingly. 'All right! I'm furious with him, but if you're so stupid that you've allowed him to seduce you, then that's just your hard luck! I came to warn you. I can see that I'm too late.'

When she had gone, the car tyres screeching at her wild take-off, Charlotte went slowly to the kitchen to find Essie.

'Essie, where exactly is Galveston?' she asked in a voice that she controlled to the point of indifference.

'It's on the Gulf, Miss Charlotte. Mr Kit has an apartment there. It's close enough to the oilfields, so he spends a lot of time there. He don't like to stay in hotels.'

Charlotte nodded and left. No, he wouldn't like to stay in hotels. He was too well known. She wandered out into the garden, her mind utterly closed to hope. It had been laid down clearly. Now it only remained to tell Kit and go home. She had to get away while she could, and if necessary she would appeal to Brett, put her pride on the line.

She had never wandered through the grounds before and, gradually, as the warmth of the late afternoon soothed her, she walked by the creek, skirting the woodland that grew well away from the house and Essie's prying eyes.

She loved it here. She admitted it. She loved Kit too, more than she could ever have imagined love to be. After that night there would be no forgetting for her.

Her mind had warned her at the time, but she had ignored it. Kit had not allowed her time to listen to it. Things like that meant nothing to a man, and she had been there, available. Tears flooded her eyes and fell in streams down her cheeks, tears she had been fending off for two days. What had it been on his part but lust, after all? He had deliberately seduced her with no thought for her.

She lay back, curling up on the short, green grass by the edge of the trees, the gurgle of the creek not now soothing but a memory she would hold for the rest of her life. Tension and pain drained away as she closed her eyes, her arm across her hot, tear-stained face as she fell asleep.

It was the sound of the boat that woke her, the bright red boat that Kit could handle like a maniac, and at first she lay there still and dazed. It was nothing to do with her, after all. She closed her eyes again, but the sound of the boat thudding into the bank brought her back to wakefulness with a snap, although she had no time to rise before Kit towered over her, his lean face white and angry.

'What the hell do you think you're doing?' he asked hoarsely, his whole body tight with suppressed feelings. 'I've been up and down the creek looking for you! Brett and Don are searching the woods! I expected to find your body in the water, you half-witted little . . . I bet you can't swim, either,' he suddenly added wildly, a growl of annoyance leaving him when she shook her head numbly.

Why was he so angry? She had every right to wander about the estate. Tears filled her eyes again as she remembered why she was here, and he seemed to notice her tear-stained face all at once.

He slid to the grass beside her and reached for her, pulling her into his arms.

'God, I thought I'd lost you!' he said savagely, his tight arms hurting her. You've got to talk to me, Charley,' he continued, his hands roughly smoothing her hair, not allowing her head to lift from his shoulder. 'But not now, not now,' he sighed. 'Any moment and Brett's going to come bursting through the woods. Anyway, you look as if you could do with a quick shower and a brandy.'

He stood, lifting her and striding to the boat, and she suddenly came to life, shuddering to feel his arms around her, a luxury she could no longer afford.

'I can walk back!' She struggled, but only briefly, because he tightened her to him fiercely.

'Charley, honey! *Please!*' he grated, and she supposed she had caused enough worries for one day. Also, she couldn't understand his great agitation.

He put her in the boat, starting the engine, and then using the horn so loudly and suddenly that she almost jumped out of her skin.

'Signalling Brett,' he said briefly, his tight face relaxing into a wry smile. 'Serves you right, honey. You deserve some kind of punishment for causing this havoc. Brett's going to rave at you. He thought his delicious new granddaughter had skipped!'

'I'm going to,' she whispered to herself, but he heard her.

'Not while I draw breath, my darling!' he said grimly, his eyes narrowed on the shining water and the approaching boathouse.

Being in a tornado must be awful, Charlotte decided later as Kit left the room and went to get her a coffee to add to the brandy he had already forced into her. She had been 'seen to' with a suppressed violence that made her feel as if she had been in a storm. Kit had marched into the house carrying her, scattering Essie before him, allowing no question and no words. Charlotte had been placed in the bathroom and threatened with instant action if she was not out and showered in ten seconds flat. He had been waiting by the door, whipping the towel away and fastening her into her robe before a blush could even surface.

She felt breathless and bemused, but ringing at the back of her mind were two small words: 'my darling'. Had he meant it? Why had he said it? A faint trickle of hope tried to fight its way to the surface, but she sternly pushed it back, she could not allow herself to hope, not yet.

There was a faint tap on the door and Brett came in, his eyes watchful as he saw her sitting on the edge of the bed. Apparently he could see no mark on her that would excuse her, and he growled at her as if she was Kit.

'Hell and damnation, Charley!' he bit out furiously. 'You came close to giving me a heart attack! You want rid of me, girl?'

She shook her head, biting her lips together to stop the laugh that tried to bubble up inside her, and his eyes narrowed just like Kit's.

'One of these days . . .' he threatened, sitting beside her and giving her a great bear-hug.

'What was it all about, then?' he asked after a minute, when she felt that if he didn't stop rocking her so violently she would be seasick. 'Were you running away from Kit?'

'No, I don't think I could do that at all,' she said in a soft murmur. 'I've thought about it, but I love him!'

He gave a great sigh of satisfaction, leaning back to look at her closely.

'Then what were you doing there, all by yourself? Essie said you looked as if you'd been crying for hours. You still look like that,' he added fiercely, looking into her eyes. He took her hand. 'I guess you'd better tell me all about it!'

For a minute she couldn't think what to say. In fact, she felt treacherous, but Brett had no power in his face now, only a deep and kindly affection, and she knew that she would have to find out about Veronica and her place in Kit's life if she was ever to be either happy or free.

'I want you to tell me about Veronica Collins!' She blurted it out before she could change her mind, and his face tightened at once.

'She's been giving you trouble, Charlotte?' he grated.

'She's been trying to, and I don't know now what to think. I know so very little, and Kit never talks about anything of his past life.'

It was hard to tell Brett half a story, and for the life of her she could not give Kit away, she could not tell his grandfather how Kit had tricked her to give him cover for seeing Veronica. She had to sort out the lies from the truth, though.

'You could ask him,' Brett murmured, his intent gaze on her face.

'No! No, I can't!'

'In case he tells you that it's all true?' he asked astutely.

She nodded. 'That and the fact that I feel that I have no right to—to . . .'

'You're his wife, Charlotte!' he said bitingly. 'Does he make you feel that you have no rights?' He sounded furious with Kit, and she hastily corrected him.

'Oh, no! It's just that—that . . .'

'All right, all right!' He patted her hand. 'You're very young for someone like Kit, I suppose. Being English and all, I expect that you're bound to feel a little out of things as yet, especially with his job calling him off and away so very often.' He glanced at her anxious face and smiled ruefully. 'All right my dear, I'll tell you about Veronica Collins, though mind you, I could get high blood-pressure just saying the name! The woman's been a thorn in the flesh since she first came to Chesapeake!'

He got up and started striding round, his temper obviously growing, but he talked and that was all she wanted.

'Eric and Kit were like brothers,' he told her. 'His family didn't have the wealth that we had, but it didn't matter at all. We hoped that when he left law school he would come straight into the business. In fact, it had been talked over for years. Then Veronica moved here with her family; her mother was a real hard case! Kit was in his late twenties, Eric younger, and he fell for Veronica like a lunatic!'

'Kit did?' Charlotte whispered, her face white.

'God, no! Kit has always been sharp! He saw her coming a mile off! No, honey, Eric fell for her charms. Kit foolishly tried to warn him, because it was Kit she was after—Kit had the money and more to come. But he was merely polite to her, for Eric's sake. She didn't stop trying, though, playing one off against the other until finally Eric joined a law firm and refused to join us. It was never out in the open, you understand, Charlotte; nobody wanted to hurt anyone else, except that woman; *she* wanted to hurt Kit!

'Finally, she married Eric, but it didn't stop her from still trying for Kit every time she got the chance, and in the end Kit stopped inviting Eric to Markland at all, it was too much of an embarrassment. That's about all, except that he went to Europe, and on the way he got himself a beautiful little wife!'

He smiled at her happily, but she was not even then convinced.

'She said that Kit married me to get back at her,' she said quietly, jumping at his explosion of sound.

'The bitch!' He glared at Charlotte, making her cringe. 'She's still at it, then? I thought as much! Listen, Charley, there has never been anything at all between that woman and Kit!'

'So they've never stayed at Kit's apartment in Galveston together?' Charlotte said faintly, and he took pity on her, breaking out into one of his great laughs.

'Kit's probably thought of taking her there to strangle her! The only reason he holds his tongue is so that Eric won't be hurt, but I think that Eric has had about enough, anyway. I've been working on Eric and, honey, when I work on somebody, they're *worked on*! I want him for the South American office. Things go wrong there and I could do with Eric.'

'Isn't that separating a man from his wife?' Charlotte asked, asked, a bit Miss Prim again in spite of his dislike of Veronica.

'No, Charley, that's separating a man from his nightmare! If she cares about him, she'll follow him. If she doesn't care, he'll know at last! Life is short, Charley, and life is sweet! Kit has got himself a whole barrelful of the sweetness in you!'

Kit strode in at that moment, and he seemed to be burning with a great satisfaction.

'I've just had Eric on the phone! He's made his mind up at last, you'll be pleased to hear! He's joining the firm! He's taking the South American job, starting next month.'

They seemed to spend a great deal of time congratulating themselves, and suddenly Kit's eyes came to Charlotte, a little warily.

'We've wanted Eric in the firm for simply ages!' he told her quietly, bringing her into this family discussion very carefully.

'Brett's been telling me,' she said softly, trying to make herself look straight at him. She wasn't yet easy in her mind and, in any case, it might mean nothing, there were other factors, after all.

'He's a good lawyer, company law. We can trust him completely!' Kit said with an embarrassed look at her, no doubt thinking of trust as being a little short where he was. 'We need him.'

'I see!' Charlotte realised that her face was stiff. She had been withdrawn with Kit since he had come in, and she simply could not help it.

Kit had needed her. Veronica had been lying, but Kit had never said anything other than that he wanted her to get Veronica off his back. It seemed to be true.

'Er—I'll go and find Essie,' Brett said abruptly, no doubt anxious about the way they just stared at each other like enemies. 'Don't you worry about that woman, Charley!' he said as he left.

Kit's eyes cooled considerably, and he closed the door behind his grandfather with a good deal of deliberation.

'You talked to Brett? Helping you has always been my prerogative. Have you got a new friend now?'

'I wanted to know—to know . . .'

'Go on, Charley!' he advised, looking down at her, his body seemingly poised on the brink of violence.

'I had to ask him something,' she said in a whisper, longing now to be back in his arms.

'Not something that you could have asked me?'

'I—I—no!' She turned away, not letting him see her face.

'I came to England and captured you, and now I'm paying the full price. Did he refuse to help you to run away?'

'I wasn't going to run away. At least . . .' She spun round and looked at him in anger, but her anger soon changed to bewilderment at the look on his face. He looked stricken, bereft, his face tight with pain.

'What did you want, then?'

'I wanted to know about Veronica. She came today. She said that you and she . . . She said that you would go to her. I know now that it wasn't true, that you told me the truth when you said you wanted to marry me for Eric's sake, to—to keep her away.'

He had stepped close and she looked up at him, her eyes searching his face.

'I'm sorry I didn't trust you, Kit,' she whispered. 'If you want me to go now—now that everything's all right about Eric, then I'm not about to make any trouble when you—you send me away.'

For a moment he just looked at her, his eyes almost shocked, and then he turned away, walking to the window, his back stiff and tense.

'Send you away?' he muttered. 'You'd have to beg me to do that, Charley!'

'If—if Brett's worrying you . . .' she began, but he turned on her savagely.

'Damn Brett!' he snarled. 'Brett's got nothing to do with this, with us.' He walked back, looking down at her. 'Do you hate me, Charley? Do you hate me for what I did to you the other night?'

She shook her head, blushing and refusing to look up.

'Whatever you told Brett, I know why you've been so miserable since then, so quiet. I had no right . . .'

'It—it just happened . . .'

'It did not just happen!' he ground out. 'I made it happen! I deliberately seduced you because I wanted you and I was scared that you'd leave me. I wanted you here for good, and now look at you, a bewildered, captured little bird—all that fight gone out of you! And don't apologise for not trusting me, Charlotte. I've lied to you from the beginning, told you every tale I could come up with just to get you here, just to marry you!' He sounded so filled with self-disgust, and her head shot up in amazement.

'But—but Uncle Joe . . . ?'

'Uncle Joe!' he muttered, sitting beside her and taking her hands in an iron grip. 'You were right long ago, Charley! We needed Joe! Brett sent me out to get him. Oh, he did all the things I've told you, but we needed him badly for something more important to us than a few dollars. We've got a field that's almost untamable—if Joe can't tame it then we'll shut down. He's got the last word!'

'But . . . but you've hidden him in Alaska!' Charlotte said. She felt dazed with relief, unable to take everything in.

'No, Charley,' Kit said softly. 'He's in the Gulf. He knows where you are and Brett knows *who* you are. I asked him not to say. Anyway,' he added wryly, 'I got a real rocket for giving Joe the push about the gambling. Didn't I tell you he's Brett's old buddy? When we found that we couldn't get anyone else for a field that's full of dangerous gas pockets, uncertain rock crevices, Brett was saying "I told you so" for weeks and weeks. I would have walked across the Atlantic to get Joe back!' He looked at her with a look that was almost humble. 'I didn't know he had a niece,' he murmured.

'So I came in useful, too,' Charlotte said softly, 'to keep Eric on your side, for the firm to . . .'

'No!' He jerked her towards him fiercely. 'God! Have I told so many lies that I'll never be able to get myself out of them?'

'Just—just tell me the truth now, she said tremulously, beginning to set free the little hope, to let it rise upwards.

For a second he looked at her, and then he pulled her to him with blind urgency, his hard lips seeking hers, his arms tightly around her with no hope of escape for the rest of her life.

Her whole body leapt in shock as he touched her, almost as if a charge of electricity has passed between them, and he lifted his head to look down at her steadily, holding her arms, some great emotion in his face. Then he pulled her roughly back to him and caught her lips with his own, enfolding her in two strong arms, cradling her head and deepening the kiss until she trembled. It seemed that it would never end, and Charlotte forgot everything as she set free the bird of happiness and clung to him, her fingers threading into his dark hair, her body trapped in the sheer magic of his arms.

She relaxed and melted against him, and his hands moved over her slowly and deliberately, moulding her body to his until her breathing was shallow and fast, her heart hammering against his. Then he lifted his head, looking down into her dazed eyes.

'I love you, Charley,' he said huskily. 'I love you, honey! I love you so much that sometimes it almost kills me to leave you!'

'Oh, Kit!' She turned her sweet mouth up to his, and he took the gift she offered like a man worshipping at a shrine. 'I love you, too, Kit! I never want to leave you.'

Her fingers trailed across his cheek, along his tight jawline, and he crushed her to him, his heart pounding against hers.

'I never thought I'd hear it, Charley!' he muttered harshly. 'I never thought you'd ever say that to me. I always thought you hated me. I've treated you so badly!'

* * *

Later, as she lay curled against him, she told him about Veronica's visit, all that Brett had said about Veronica, and he grunted angrily.

'I've put up with that woman for long enough, and you know, deep down, I have this feeling that she loves Eric anyway. I guess she's either just plain mean or crazy. When he goes, she'll follow him, I don't doubt that at all. One thing's for sure, she'll not bother you again, my love!'

'Oh, I can handle her now, now I know that you love me,' Charlotte said, winding her arms around his neck. He laughed down at her, his looks light and happy.

'You know, I couldn't seem to keep away from you once I'd met you. I used to come into that office and face that dragon simply to get a glimpse of you. I couldn't understand why I did it! I'd ask myself what it was about you that drew me there, and you never even noticed that I was alive!'

'I was too scared to look up!' Charlotte protested. 'When you asked me to have lunch I was furious. I thought you were up to no good!'

'I was,' he admitted, grinning down at her. 'I was working out how to get you!'

'You were waiting to get to Uncle Joe!' she reminded him sternly, but he shook his head.

'I'd almost forgotten Joe by then, honey,' he confessed. 'Then you came tearing into my flat, all wet and anxious, straight into the trap! I had you and Joe at one fell swoop.'

'You're ruthless!' Charlotte accused, her grey eyes dangerously sparkling, but he only nodded happily.

'I had to be,' he confessed softly. 'Look where it got me! You rocked me out of my mind, especially with that wet blouse,' he added, grinning at her blushes.

'Is that when you fell in love with me?' she asked

shyly, and he laughed delightedly.

'No, honey! I guess I fell in love with you when you turned on me the first day we met. I got a good lecture, got good and mad, and then love hit me like a hammer!'

'You didn't believe in love,' Charlotte reminded him softly.

'Charley, I'm going to have to stop lying,' he said humbly. 'You'll have to help me.'

'You can bank on that!' Charlotte said severely. 'If Brett knew all this and kept quiet too, then he's just as bad. I'm not having our children brought up telling suave lies!'

'Say that again, darling,' he breathed, tightening his arms around her.

'About lies?' she asked, astonished.

'About children. Do you want to, Charley?'

'Yes!' she whispered, burying her suddenly hot face against him.

They both turned astonished faces to the door as, with a brief knock, Brett walked into the room, looking decidedly abashed as he saw them lying on top of the bed with their arms tightly around each other.

'Hell's teeth! I'm sorry!' he muttered, beating a hasty retreat.

Kit rolled off the bed and scooped Chrlotte into his arms, making rapidly for the door.

'That just about does it!' he muttered. 'In future, Mrs Landor, you'll sleep in my bed, then maybe we'll get less visiting! It's a good job we hadn't got any further!' he said, sliding her to her feet in his room, closing the door firmly and locking it with a satisfied look at the big, old lock. 'Friends, Charley?' he asked softly, his hands tenderly on her, his eyes brilliantly blue as they looked into hers.

'Friends, Kit,' she said tremulously, her face glowing

with happiness.

'And lovers, Charley,' he whispered against her lips. 'Always lovers!'

'Always,' she agreed softly as he gathered her close to the hard safety of his body, his warmth and desire driving away every last doubt.

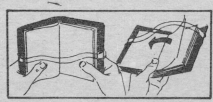
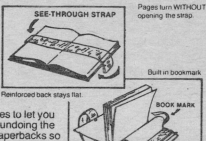